Advance Praise for *For Such a Time as This*

'Shani Akilah is a glittering new voice in the literary firmament. With insight and compassion she gets under the skin and inside the messy relationships of millennials in a way that feels vital and fresh.'
Bernardine Evaristo, author of *Girl, Woman, Other*, winner of the Booker Prize

'Set against the backdrops of London, Ghana and Jamaica, Shani has produced the paginated equivalent of that first toe dipping into a steaming bath – a sparkling, thought-provoking debut collection full of warmth, that gingerly guides you through the turmoil of the pandemic and sits you at the intersection of love, grief, uncertainty and the tender bonds of friendship and family.'
Onyi Nwabineli, author of *Allow Me to Introduce Myself*

'*For Such a Time as This* is like one of those amazing, timeless albums where any song you select, you're guaranteed to enjoy it. All the stories are heartachingly beautiful. You'll have this book on repeat!'
Lizzie Damilola Blackburn, author of *Yinka, Where is Your Huzband?*

'I raced through these moreish, tender and thoroughly engrossing slices of contemporary life exploring love, loss, friendship, and the people and places we call home. There's a warm and heartfelt quality to Shani's writing that makes this collection difficult to put down.'
Jyoti Patel, author of *The Things That We Lost*

'I devoured this in one day. This is such a special collection of stories, like a time capsule of young, Black British London life suffused with love and warmth.'

Jendella Benson, author of *Hope & Glory*

'*For Such a Time as This* is a collection that, like its stories, leaves one wanting more. Readers are taken on a round-trip journey briefly but intensely through the full range of human emotions. It is a beautiful, gripping and humorously vivid work that puts Southeast Londoners on the map, and for that we are grateful and proud!'

Nikki Adebiyi, founder of Bounce Black

'A rich collection of stories that are visceral, thought-provoking and convey every human emotion. Shani Akilah is a stunning and exciting new voice and a writer to watch.'

Nadine Matheson, author of *The Jigsaw Man*

'Eloquent, accessible, and full of heart, these interconnected stories draw one into an unforgettable group of young, Black-British friends. Funny, thought provoking and deeply moving. An astonishing debut.'

Taiye Selasi, author of *Ghana Must Go*

FOR SUCH A TIME AS THIS

SHANI AKILAH

MAGPIE
BOOKS

A Magpie Book

First published in the United Kingdom, Republic of Ireland and Australia
by Magpie Books, an imprint of Oneworld Publications, 2024

Copyright © Shani Akilah, 2024

The moral right of Shani Akilah to be identified as the Author of
this work has been asserted by her in accordance with the Copyright,
Designs and Patents Act 1988

ISBN 978-0-86154-692-3
eISBN 978-0-86154-693-0

Typeset by Hewer Text Ltd, Edinburgh
Printed and bound in Great Britain by Clays Ltd, Elcograf S.p.A

Excerpt from 'Diaspora Blues' by Ijeoma Umebinyuo, taken
from the collection *Questions for Ada*, copyright © 2015 by Ijeoma
Umebinyuo. Cited with permission of the author.

Oneworld Publications
10 Bloomsbury Street
London WC1B 3SR
England

Stay up to date with the latest books,
special offers, and exclusive content from
Oneworld with our newsletter

Sign up on our website
oneworld-publications.com

MIX
Paper | Supporting
responsible forestry
FSC® C018072

To my grandparents, Hyacinth, Roy,
Phyllis and Reginald, thank you for everything.

CONTENTS

vii

INTRO: THE COMMUTE

It is the first week back after the slowed indulgence between Christmas and New Year, forgetting what day it is.

Movie marathons, vision board-making and impromptu gatherings with friends are no more. Instead, you're joining the stream of commuters at Woolwich Arsenal, lightly tapping your bank card on the Oyster reader, its coral hue standing out amidst the crowd. On the escalator you do not stand but walk briskly down the left-hand side, a stark contrast to the leisurely rhythm of the previous day. Arriving on the lower ground, the platform is packed. But after three years of making this journey, you know exactly where you need to stand to get a seat.

The train is due in three minutes, so you open your bag and take out *Children of Virtue and Vengeance*, the January pick for the book club you co-run. Once on the carriage, you nestle into your preferred seat, ready to delve into the next chapter. But just before the door closes, you see a woman with a BABY ON BOARD badge. The man sitting next to you with AirPods fixed in his ears pretends not to see her. The woman opposite has her eyes shut, a scarf wrapped around her face – a clear signal that her daily twenty-seven-minute power nap to Bank is not to be interrupted. No one readily offers their seat; the holiday season of good-will is a distant memory. You stand, picking up your book and your bag, and give up your seat with a smile. You then take hold of the pole opposite with one hand.

No longer seated, you struggle to read as the driverless train jerks and twists along the meandering tracks of random stops through East London. You close your book, missing your usual twelve minutes of solace between your local station and Canning Town. Your eyes are taking in the outside views, dotted with dilapidated factories, when you spot a flash of red and orange on the far right of the carriage. The colours are overlaid with black and white, a tapestry of lines and curves. It is the front cover of your favourite book, the interwoven story of two sisters and their descendants, spanning multiple generations, each chapter part of the puzzle of connections past and present, from the motherland to the diaspora. It is the book that made you fall in love with fiction again after years of reading only journal articles and textbooks at university. You are intrigued. Your favourite book is in the hands of a man. Most of your male friends seem to read only biographies and self-help books. But the man before you is more than halfway through the most beautiful novel you have ever read. You are overcome with the desire to speak to him. You consider telling him about your Black women's book club and the next biannual session, where you invite men to join the conversation. You think of his potential insights. Of what he might say. Of the contributions he could add to the meeting. But the train is packed. Maybe if you manoeuvre yourself closer to him, you could catch his eye. But he is immersed. Minutes go by and he doesn't look up once.

There is a gradual slowing down of the train. The man begins to stand. You're also getting off at the next station and decide that if you are quick enough, you can walk beside him as he leaves the carriage. Your mind scans through some potential conversation starters about the book he's still holding. The doors open with a piercing shriek, and he takes a few steps forward. Just as you have decided what to say and have started edging towards the door, there is a tap on your shoulder.

You turn around and see a woman pointing to a strip of kente cloth on the floor. Your newest bookmark has fallen out of your novel. You reach down to pick it up and say thank you, and then leave the train, trying to find the man who is holding your favourite book. But he has disappeared, is nowhere to be seen. You begin your walk to

Platform 4 for the Jubilee Line, the final leg of your journey. You think maybe you will see him, but there are so many people awaiting the train that is due in two minutes. You scan the orderly lines of city workers, engrossed in their phones and holding newspapers collected from previous journeys. You can't see him. He could be anywhere. You realise it is an impossible task, and think it is a little creepy anyway. Instead, you make your way to the far end of the platform.

On board the second packed train of the morning, you reach for your phone. You open WhatsApp, home to the many group chats you have created over the years. A date has been agreed for your regular link-up with your friends from university. In another, your childhood friend sends her apologies and says she can't make brunch this month because of work. On iMessage, your work friends confirm that they are free to meet for lunch at one. You have just liked a post on Instagram, a reminder of the upcoming twenty-one days of prayer and fasting at your church, when the Tube arrives at Canary Wharf. The doors open and there is a mass exodus, freeing up seats for you to sit down at last and return to your book.

As the Tube rattles through the various stations towards Central London, you look at the pages of your novel, but you are not taking in the words. You are thinking about the man who was reading your favourite book. You think that if the train hadn't been as busy, not packed with people like sardines, you might have been able to reach him. That maybe if he and you had been sitting opposite each other, you might have been able to have a conversation. You think such a meeting could be the prologue to a wonderful story. A Black British romcom version of *The Girl on the Train*, but with a twist: *The Man on the Train with a Book*. You make a mental note for inspiration for a future short story, thinking of your New Year's resolution of returning to your hobby of creative writing. And then, you return to reality. You return to your book.

You've read another ten pages when you hear the familiar announcement: 'The doors will open on the right-hand side. Change for the Bakerloo, Northern, Waterloo and City, and National Rail services.' Though it is not yet your stop, for some reason you look up and out to the platform. You see him. He sees you. The book is still in his hands. He smiles. And then the doors shut.

The train is moving again. You feel something akin to loss, though you don't even know this man's name. You don't know anything about him. A gentle sigh escapes you and then you close your novel. You unwrap your silk scarf, revealing your now slicked edges and faux locs gathered together on your right shoulder. You open your bag, take out your work pass and bank card and tuck away your scarf and book. And then comes the announcement you haven't heard since last year: 'The next station is Westminster. Exit here for the Houses of Parliament and Westminster Abbey.'

You depart the Tube and leave the platform via a side exit. You walk up three sets of escalators, weaving through tourists peppered throughout the station, many of whom stand on the left despite continual reminders to stand on the right-hand side. After tapping out, irked by commuters who fail to pre-emptively retrieve their cards from wallets before arriving at the barriers, you leave the station. In the underpass you stop and chat to the *Big Issue* seller for a little while. He comments like he always does on your smile, asks you about your Christmas break, and you wish each other a good day. You are disappointed not to see the Jamaican man with his guitar. He only ever plays a Bob Marley medley, but without fail he will interrupt his song as you pass to call out, 'Hello, my sistah,' a greeting that always brightens your morning.

Outside, you walk towards your place of work. At the entrance, you show your pass to the security guard, a formality because he knows your face. You wish each other a happy new year. You enter the building and walk through the gate, where on the other side of the barrier you see another of the many Black security guards that you talk to. He says it's good to see you and wishes you good health and prosperity, especially prosperity, for 2020.

Inside the lift on your way to the fourth floor of the building, you think back to the man with your favourite book. You wonder if you will ever see him again. There are, after all, five days in which you go into the office. And after a much-needed break, you are back to your nine-to-five. Back to the routine of it all, another year waiting to be wrapped in a Spotify playlist.

GOOD GOODBYE

For Gabby, 2021 was the year *everyone* got married. It was the year of proposals, engagement parties, weddings and posts on the Gram captioned *I said yes to my best friend* and *Here's to forever with the love of my life.* It was the year she was asked to be a bridesmaid not once, not twice, but six times for friends from school, university and summer internships. It was the year aunties held her close and whispered, 'Don't worry, my dear, you are next' and 'Your huzband is coming o.'

But by year two of the pandemic, Gabby had completed her rebrand. She was no longer the sort of person who caught feelings, she caught flights. She was a 'girlboss' now, part of the 'men are trash' contingent, with no time for romantic attachments, only for securing the bag. She found the idea of being caught up in another person's needs, their wants and insecurities, insufferable. To her, it was a sickness that got in the way of ambition. In all aspects, falling in love was a grave distraction. And she had things to do.

Nevertheless, she had her #BridesmaidDuties on lock and put her corporate training to good use, treating each wedding like a work project. She had an Excel spreadsheet of the best vendors for bridal shower balloon arches, and she knew where to obtain additional special touches like natural blush-pink pampas grass or a personalised banner with a matching cake stand. She knew where to source champagne satin robes with BRIDE SQUAD embroidered across the back for hen weekends, and where to get custom-made flute glasses for pre-drinks before the big day. She knew of the make-up artists who would have your face beat, giving you a soft glam look, versus the ones who went too hard on the contour and left you looking like a Bratz doll. She had on speed dial the stylists she found on Instagram who would have your edges laid and form a perfectly slicked high ponytail. If there was an award for best bridesmaid of the year, it would go to her every single time. To everyone that knew her, she was absolutely boss-ing this chapter of her life, like everything else she did.

As Wedding Number Five drew to an end though, and she watched her closest friend from law school begin her first dance with her now-husband, her stomach sank, her throat grew tight. The song that filled the room had once lived in a playlist. A playlist she had deleted years ago. It was a reminder of a life before the one she knew now. Of love, of butterflies and feeling intoxicated with joy. But then of happiness turned bad, corrupted. Before the song had reached its chorus, she disappeared into the bathroom, where she locked herself in a cubicle and cried.

For Jonathan, wedding season was also seasoning. Though not playing the role of serial groomsman or best man, he spent most weekends during the summer driving up and down the M25, attending weddings in Braintree, St Albans and Chelmsford. For him, weddings were an opportunity for enjoyment with the mandem, for dancing and drinking and getting pictures for the Gram, which he captioned *Wedding Season* 🎉🏠. He was often the life of the party, bringing energy to the dance floor and hyping up the groom as the DJ transitioned into the funky house set, reliving moments from their secondary school days. He was also the resident joker. The one to clear his throat as the wedding officiator asked if there was anyone who did not believe that these two people should be joined. And he was the first, along with his boys, to jump on the revolving video booth that spun at 360 degrees. The 120 frames that were captured in slow motion – the latest craze of the summer – would later be titled #WeddingEnjoyment on Twitter. For him, life was about working hard and playing harder. And weddings were a prime opportunity to get lit.

But this wedding was different. He had been invited at the last minute by his university friend David. It was a rare weekend where he wasn't attending a day party, barbecue or impromptu games night, and so he turned up to the wedding even though he did not know the bride or groom in any depth. In his usual fashion, he arrived late, minutes before the bridal party entered the church.

And it was at that moment that he saw her.

A drowning sensation overcame him, making him feel as if he were losing control of his body. Somehow, despite moving in similar circles, he'd managed to avoid her over the last few years. But he'd always known this day would come. Like him, she was bait. But he did not think he would see her like this, ready to begin her descent down the aisle with the rest of the bridal party as the bride followed in their wake. But there she was, after what seemed like a lifetime, dressed in sunshine. She looked like a goddess: her ebony hair was longer than he remembered, and glowed in the natural light. Her body was more womanly now, her bum and breasts more accentuated. But just like the first time he'd met her, her smile was still the most perfect curve on her frame. He felt his stomach clench. She was the one who had said goodbye to him years ago and never looked back.

Five years earlier, Gabby was sitting in a pub, waiting. The setting made her skin crawl – its alcohol-saturated carpet and the smell of spirits mixed with must and wood. The walls were the colour of vomit, and grey mould crept up towards the ceiling. If the location wasn't confirmation enough, when he arrived minutes after the agreed time, his outfit, a dark grey tracksuit, signalled that this certainly was not a date. She had arrived early as usual and was dressed in a beige blazer with blue jeans and heeled ankle boots. He had always valued comfort over the drip. It was something she still admired about him.

Jonathan took a seat opposite Gabby, leaving the chair next to her vacant. 'So, here we are,' he said. There were no pleasantries. No babe. No baby. No Gabs.

'Here we are indeed,' said Gabby, tired.

He was tired too.

'How was your birthday?' she asked. A few months ago, she had planned to go over and above, as she had done in previous years. A surprise party with his closest friends. A video message montage. Dinner at Gaucho. She had even thought about a city break somewhere in Europe. But when it came to it, she had just sent a generic *happy birthday* text, which he responded to more than twelve hours later. No emojis. No love hearts. No Gabs.

'Yeah, it was really nice, thanks,' he said with a smile that cut Gabby deep. It was another 21 November where she had cried herself to sleep, her pillow soaked in a mix of snot and cream for her acne. She hated how her love for him made her so weak. So out of control. So vulnerable.

'So, how do you want to do this then?' said Jonathan, leaning back in his chair. He removed his puffa jacket and took out his phone. Then he scrolled to his notes app ready to begin his soliloquy.

Gabby pulled in her chair and pushed her glasses up her nose. 'To be honest with you, Jonathan, I don't think there's any point in us going into it all. We've been here so many times before.' And it was true; she felt like she had lived this a hundred times.

Jonathan noted that Gabby had her serious face on.

'We tried,' she continued. 'We tried so hard again. And it hasn't worked. I think we just need to be cool with that.'

He sighed, deeping it all. 'You're right,' he lied. He believed that this time they could work it out. He knew what he needed to do. Instead, he locked his phone and put it back into his pocket. 'Why meet up then? We could have just spoken on the phone, no?'

Gabby looked at the surroundings, her eyes taking in the run-down pub. 'Closure, I guess,' she said with a faint smile, thinking about a tweet she had seen that claimed the 'C' word was in fact a scam. She had come to the decision weeks ago. She had told her girls in their group chat. She had even written a letter to her future self. And then in her journal that evening, she'd written down Maya Angelou's words about believing people the first time they show you who they really are. She had agreed in advance that there was nothing he could say to change her mind. She could not enter another year like this. She had things to do. She had a plan for her career. She had a plan for her life. She needed it to be a clean break. Free from inconsistency and ambiguity. She needed to put herself first, leaving behind ideas of what he could be at the altar. She was done. Finished. For real this time.

In the toilets, Gabby tried to rectify the damage to her smudged make-up. She opened her clutch bag and located her MAC Dark Deep powder, which she used to pat under her eyes. She leaned further into the mirror and said, 'Hold it together, sis, you've got this.' She recited her morning affirmations: 'I am strong, I am powerful, I can do anything I want to do if I put my mind to it.' Taking out a worn toothbrush from her bag to touch up her edges, she whispered, 'Don't let him get in your head. You've come so far.' She then used the corner of her longer-than-usual almond-shaped nail to neaten the eyeliner that had run slightly. She took a deep breath and smoothed down the mustard silk that hugged her hips, turning to view her side profile that had become more pronounced over the last few months – a result of her personal trainer's insistence on squats and dead lifts. 'You've got this,' she said again. Then she left the bathroom and made her way to the dance floor, following the afrobeats blaring from the hallway.

Hours before, Jonathan had tried to keep himself inconspicuous. He had decided to keep a low profile, to not be seen by her. When David asked wagwan for him, questioning his unusually quiet demeanour, he lied and said he'd had a late night and was tired. Despite his best efforts to forget Gabby, he could not keep his eyes off her. He had watched as she walked down the aisle, her hand interlocked in an arm that wasn't his. He noticed that her nails were longer, painted burgundy, his favourite colour. He had seen the tear that had fallen from her eye as the bride cried whilst repeating 'I promise to love and cherish and honour you' and tried to find a tissue in her bag. He observed from afar how she was starting to get tired from taking back-to-back pictures in the outside grounds, eyeing the canapés of vegetable spring rolls and plantain bruschetta as they passed. He noted that she looked slightly uncomfortable with the dance routine as the bridal party entered the reception, but that she had given it her all. And so of course he'd noticed when she'd got up and left at the sounds of the song that had once featured on their shared Spotify playlist. The playlist she had deleted.

Five years before, in the pub with its alcohol-saturated carpet, Gabby and Jonathan stood up. She took hold of her coat and bag. He always travelled light, so had to wait for what felt like hours whilst she got herself together. They walked to the door. He opened it for her.

'Did you get the Tube?' Jonathan asked as they stood

outside the Royal Oak, somewhere Gabby already knew she'd never return to.

'Nah, the DLR. Where did you park?'

'Just a few roads away,' he said.

Normally he would have dropped her home. Normally they would have stayed in his car for hours, parked not far from her parents' house, talking, laughing and sharing kisses.

A strained silence lingered between them.

'Bye Gabby,' said Jonathan, reaching out for an embrace. She put her arms out towards him. They hugged. He smelt like caramel and Hugo Boss. She smelt the same as she did when they had first met at sixteen, her natural scent infused with the Britney Spears Midnight perfume that always reminded him of the Gabs who knew exactly what she wanted in life, even then. He had so much to say, but when he opened his mouth all that came was, 'Gabs, I honestly do wish you well in everything.'

'Same, Jon,' she said, her eyes filling up.

Despite the pain, she did love him deeply. But she needed to love herself more. She wasn't going to cry. That was what she had done last time, and the time before. She pulled away from him and fixed her scarf, which was now lopsided.

'Bye, Jonathan,' Gabby said and turned to begin her walk to the station, tears streaming down her face. She wasn't going to let him see her cry. Instead she texted her girls' group chat and said it was done. This was goodbye. For real this time. There would be no turning back for her.

Jonathan watched as Gabby left her table at the sound of the song they had once shared. It reminded him of the time when he'd half hoped she would turn back. How he'd wished she would have heard what he'd planned to say to her. How he had stood there for what felt like an eternity, watching her leave his life forever. He still thought about that moment from time to time. It lived rent-free in his heart and mind; it lived in his guilt. He knew that, for good or ill, she had been the making of him. That she was a woman he would never forget. Sometimes in bed at night, his mind would return to the pub, wondering if he could have done anything differently. Whether he could have apologised. Whether he could have declared that he could be the man she needed him to be, though he knew this wasn't true. Whether he could have told the truth and said she was the only woman who really understood him. Whether he would have let her slip away so easily. But he reasoned that this was life. That there were things far worse things than heartbreak.

After the DJ finished the highlife set and the bridesmaids had flocked to the dance floor, picking up US dollars sprayed by aunties onto the newly-wed couple, Gabby walked over to the open bar at the back of the venue. She had been tasked with getting drinks for herself and the maid of honour, who had plans to get the videographer into bed after the night had ended. 'Can I get two rum and Cokes please?' she said at the bar.

Jonathan heard her before he saw her. And then she saw him.

He felt the sudden drowning sensation again. She felt her heart stop.

Together, they stood steps away from each other, the closest they had been since they had left the pub five years before. It was too late for Jonathan not to say anything now. 'Hey, Gabby,' he said, his voice barely audible.

Of all the places Gabby had thought she would see him, she hadn't thought it would be here. Years ago she had made up different scenarios of what she would say, what she would do. She said she would play it cool. Show him that she was good, that she had moved on with her life. 'Jonathan,' she said, forgetting her lines. She should have been ready to say *Hey, you alright? I'm doing great, byeeee niggaaaaa* and kept it moving. But she forgot to remind him that it was Gabriella now. More professional, just like her. Instead, all she said was, 'You're here.'

'Yeah, my boy invited me,' said Jonathan with a smile, though there was nothing to smile about. He wanted the floor below his feet to swallow him whole. 'You look well,' he said. It was an understatement: she looked beautiful. Still the most beautiful woman he had ever come across.

'Thank you,' said Gabby, her eyes taking him in. She

surveyed his full black beard, the day she'd bought him organic castor oil to help with the thickness coming to mind.

His eyes were still the colour of chestnut, the first thing she had noticed when they'd met in year twelve at a conference for top Black students. After one of the sessions, entitled 'How to make the most of your time in first year', her friend Niah from sixth form had played the role of matchmaker and introduced them, realising they both had plans to study history and politics at university.

His white shirt hugged his muscles. His trim was fresh and his shape-up clean. He looked good, really good. She did not return the compliment, however, but said, 'How are you?'

'I'm well, you know,' said Jonathan. He paused for a few moments, pondering what would be the most appropriate thing to say after all these years. An awkward silence stretched between them. Gabby ran her hands through her hair, something Jonathan remembered she did when she was nervous. He caught sight again of her long, burgundy nails, which seemed to scream grown and sophisticated. Gabby opened her mouth to say something in response, but the words did not materialise. Words instead came to Jonathan and he continued, 'We've just closed our first VC round of funding, so things are quite busy.' He needed her to know that he was doing better. That his life was on track. That he was slowly becoming the man he'd known he had the potential to be but that she couldn't hang around long enough to see. Although meeting her like this had unnerved him. He didn't ask how she was doing back. He knew she was killing it. He had seen from LinkedIn, the only social media platform she hadn't blocked him from. He wondered if that was intentional. So he asked her, 'How are the fam?'

Jonathan had once been an integral part of Gabby's world, and by extension her family's world. Her loss had been theirs too. She needed to stifle the burgeoning grief, and so she answered quickly. 'They're good. Everyone's well.'

'I'm glad,' said Jonathan, realising Gabby's face was now blemish-free, no longer marked by the acne of her teens and early twenties.

Again there was a disconcerting pause. This time Gabby filled the silence and added, 'Rae-Ann's pregnant with her second. She's due any minute now actually.'

'No way! It only seems like yesterday that they got married. Wow,' said Jonathan, rather too loudly, as if to acknowledge gratitude for this extra insight into a world he was no longer part of. A memory from Gabby's sister's wedding resurfaced in Jonathan's mind. It was when he'd realised she was the one. Gabby thought of that moment too. The day when he was her plus one. Where they had danced together as teens and said it would be them one day. She wished she hadn't mentioned it.

Before either of them got a chance to fill the ever-expanding awkwardness, the MC called for all the single ladies to join the dance floor.

Jonathan looked at Gabby. Then he looked down at her hand, which was bare. He needed to know. He said, 'You next then?'

'No,' she said, embarrassed. She wished she'd been able to tell him that yes, she would soon be getting married. She wished that after all these years she'd found someone else. Someone who made her heart sing, who gave her belly laughs. But that space had been left broken, then unoccupied, despite her brief string of Tinder dates. She had never been the same since, and she hated herself because of it. 'I should go and join the girls,' she said.

'Of course. See you, Gabs,' he said in response. Despite the drowning sensation, forgetting time and space, he reached for an embrace. She moved towards him. He noticed she smelt different. She felt the contours of his back, the same but stronger. Their bodies still fitted together perfectly, like a mosaic – complete. They both felt it. The electric current that ran from him to her. 'We were kids,' he said without words.

Her spirit heard and replied: 'You weren't there when I needed you to be.'

His responded: 'No one taught me how to be a man. No one taught me how to love a woman.'

Their bodies were again two halves.

'See you, Jon.'

So much time had passed.

'See you, Gabs.'

Suddenly the music seemed louder, drowning out the silent words passing between them.

Gabby stood in line with the other unmarried bridesmaids and single women. The MC started a drawn-out countdown. Three, two, one. Gabby extended her hands to reach for the bouquet thrown in her direction by the bride. She felt the petals of the flowers brush her fingers. Without warning, another woman snatched it from her hands, eager to secure her own fate. At first, Gabby was glad. But then she felt disappointed. She looked back to the bar where she had said goodbye to the man who still held a piece of her. Part of her wanted this moment to resemble a scene from a Disney movie, where she caught the bouquet as Jonathan walked towards her. He would stand in front of her, hold her hand and say, *I have never stopped loving you. I messed up, you are mine forever. My person.* He would smile softly and continue, *I am better now, older. I know what it is to be a man, your man. I know, finally, how to love you how you want to be loved.* But she held such thoughts captive. She knew real life was not like the movies. Jonathan watched her walk away.

Later that night, when the after-party had finished and the bride and groom were in their wedding suite, the maid of honour in bed with the videographer and the other brides-maids curled up with their fiancés and boyfriends, Gabby sat alone on the double bed of her Premier Inn room. She'd removed her ponytail attachment, had taken out her contact lenses and had washed the gel out of her hair. She held her phone in her hand. Despite deleting it many years ago, she'd never succeeded in forgetting his number.

Whilst Gabby stared at the digits on her phone, Jonathan was driving, having dropped home those of his friends who'd had too much to drink. At the traffic lights, he stopped, picked up his phone and scrolled to her name. He opened up a new message. *Gabs*, he typed, *you are the only person I have ever loved*. He deleted it and typed *Hey Gabby, it was really good seeing you today. Can we talk?* He deleted that message too. Then he turned up the music and threw his phone onto the empty passenger seat.

Back in the hotel room, Gabby thought about the prom-ise she'd made to herself all those years ago. That she would not be the first to reach out. But maybe after all this time he *was* different. She told herself that they were, after all, both nearing their fourth decade. She tossed and turned. And then she broke her promise.

After some hesitation, Jonathan sent the text. But what he didn't know was that, after walking away from the pub, Gabby had blocked and deleted his number. So she didn't get the text from him. And he didn't receive the text from her. Because although she'd thought she still knew his number, she'd got the last digit wrong – a seven instead of an eight. So both texts were sent into the atmosphere, never to be seen by the person they were intended for, changing the course of their lives together and their lives apart.

In the morning, with the sun shining bright, Gabby felt better and reminded herself that her emotions could not be trusted. That decisions relating to matters of the heart should not be made during the night. She blamed it on the alcohol. She then deleted the message he had never received, as if it hadn't existed. She thought about her journal entry from all those years ago; that people don't change, not really. She recited her daily affirmations.

On his run that same morning and after he hadn't heard back from Gabby, Jonathan convinced himself that there were more important things in life. He told himself that he was still young, an eligible bachelor, the co-founder of one of the fastest growing start-ups in the country. He reminded himself that his best years were still ahead of him. That he would be good.

Years later, after people had forgotten how they had lived before everything changed, they would see each other again. Him with someone he loved but had settled for. Her with someone she also loved but who did not make her heart sing. They would smile, an ode to the love they had once shared as teens.

GHANA IN DECEMBER

David wakes up drenched in sweat, his white tee damp.

He is haunted each December by the nightmare. It replaces the dreams he doesn't remember, in the month that marks his birthday. The scene is always the same – of a car coming fast, shattering bones and obliterating a heartbeat. The body is a mirror to his own, but broken, no longer brown and beautiful, filled with joy and hope for things to come. Instead it is limp, covered in warm blood.

Sitting up on the sofa, he wipes the beads of moisture from his forehead. He needs to suppress the panic in his depths, and so he reaches for his phone. He realises it is barely 8 p.m. The nightmare has been causing insomnia, with random naps working from home during the day. He opens Instagram, prees a few stories and then uploads a picture which he captions *throwback*. He unveils to his 2,766 followers a shot of him dressed in a silk shirt, linen shorts and Ray-Ban sunglasses. He is holding the steering wheel of a yacht, which shows his once-bulging biceps. It is another image adding to his reputation as 'Mr Enjoyment', one of many in his curated feed of lifestyle and luxury. Other pictures show him perched on a white BMW 3 Series, a Rolex on his wrist and a Versace belt on full display; and further afield, outstretched on a sunlounger in Santorini. The likes cascade in with comments including *ayeee my guy* and *jheeezzz*. It feels good, but it's more than that. Beyond attempting to forget the nightmare, part of him hopes that engaging in this virtual abyss will remove what feels like darkness. But it rises to the surface.

He stands up. He walks out onto the balcony of his river-side apartment in Royal Arsenal. The balcony directly beneath him is decorated with an aloe vera plant, an outdoor sofa and a string of vintage fairy lights. He zones into a sole unlit bulb amidst the illuminated ones. He is trying to recall from secondary school physics whether it is a series or a parallel circuit. Then he walks closer to the edge of the balcony. He takes in the river beneath him, pitch-black under the night sky. The realm beyond the twenty-three storeys below. He wonders what it would mean to give himself to the water without struggle. Whether being submerged will remove the terror he is unable to shift. If maybe on the other side of water entering his lungs is freedom. He is still for some time.

His phone flashes, a glow of bright white.

It's an incoming call from Jonathan. David looks at the name for some time, thinking about the text he'd received a few days ago: *You good bro?* David had wanted to say *Nah, I'm not, I can't lie.* But he didn't reply, airing the message. He thinks now to do the same but knows Jonathan will call him again and again.

Back on the sofa, he picks up and says, 'Yoo,' to which Jonathan replies, 'My G,' in their regular greeting since meeting during Freshers' Week nearly a decade ago. 'You good?' Jonathan asks again.

David knows he is the furthest thing from good. That alongside the grey cloud that has a habit of creeping up on him during the days starved of vitamin D is not just the nightmare but the nightmare's companions, which are beginning to resurface during his unending days in his apartment-turned-office. He has no escape. He can no longer do up enjoyment, driving with the guys from motive to motive at the weekend, with nights out in Shoreditch and drink-ups in the depths of North London. He can't even go to the gym. All he can muster is, 'I'm surviving, man.'

'I hear it,' says Jonathan. 'You managing to get out of the house a bit though?'

David looks again to the balcony. 'A little bit.' Trying to change the subject, he asks, 'What about you? What you saying?'

Jonathan sighs and says, 'Life has been lifeing, you know.'

'Bro,' says David.

'Me and Emmanuel are actually thinking about going to Ghana in a few weeks, to get out of here for a while,' Jonathan says. 'I know you're not normally on it, but given Boris wants to hold us hostage again, I wondered if you'd be down?'

In previous years when Jonathan and Emmanuel had invited David to join them to turn up in the motherland at the end of the year, he'd always claimed he preferred the indulgence of Dubai: its inauthenticity, yacht parties and desert attire. Year after year he told the same lie. 'I dunno, man,' says David.

But then he thinks back to the Clubhouse room he'd been pinged into a few days before. Of how he had joined over a hundred people in the virtual space, who were discussing all things Ghana in December. How Emmanuel had brought him onto the virtual stage and asked, 'When was the last time you touched down in Accra, bro?' And he had laughed it off, saying, 'Allow me, it's been a minute,' but how he'd felt sick to his stomach. And that days later he'd found himself craving fufu and light soup and ordered it two nights in a row. And then, out of the blue, how he'd received a message from Kwaku, a cousin he hadn't seen in over fifteen years.

'Think about it though. It would be good for you to get some sun,' says Jonathan, remembering that David has declined all his suggestions of meeting up for a walk. He hesitates. 'I've been listening to this podcast recently, and it got me thinking about some stuff.' He stops. 'I honestly think my dad would be different, better, if he hadn't stayed here so long and had gone back to Sierra Leone.'

'What do you mean?' says David.

There is silence. 'I've never said . . .' says Jonathan. He stops again. 'I've never said, but my dad . . . he really struggles.' He clears his throat. 'He's had issues since I was like ten. We never spoke about it growing up.'

'Swear?' says David, though he feels a wave of nausea.

'Yeah man, schizophrenia,' says Jonathan, not using the vague wording David has seen in well-being emails at work. He is more specific, going on to speak of mania and chronic depression. Of psychotic episodes and hallucinations. He continues, his words spilling out like a flood. But there are still things he can't talk about. He doesn't mention the times where he wouldn't know which version of his father he would get when he came back from school. Of having to step up at home. Of the times he had to play the role of husband to his mother and father to his younger siblings. Of the guilt he'd felt when he had firmed the University of Warwick as his first choice, hours away from his home. 'He had a crisis a few weeks ago,' he continues, 'and it got me thinking a lot about the shit we experience. About how this country kills us in so many ways.'

Though Jonathan has spoken at length about his regrets with Gabby, his ex-girlfriend, David has never known his friend to be this open, to unravel in such a way. He wonders if it's because he's had more space to be in his thoughts, taking time to be still. But he is rattled. Triggered. He thinks of his own father. 'My dad committed suicide,' is what he wants to say, but he cannot. He wants to say that he too knows of the voices. Of the long days in bed. Of refusing to seek help but also of the services not built with us in mind. Of going missing for weeks. He wants to say that he too knows of the prayer, and the fasting that doesn't work. Of seeing your mother retreat into something you have never known her to be – weary. Of the weight of the lie, telling everyone your father died from a heart attack. He is not sure what speaking about it all will do to him. Of what it will open up. He knows that beyond the seasonal depression that plagues him each winter, beyond the microaggressions at work, beyond the back and forth with his ex-girlfriend, beyond the anger with his father and more recently his mother, lies his dead brother. It is an act of self-preservation, so none of these things he shares with Jonathan. Instead he says, 'Man, that's a lot.' He stops. 'I'm so sorry to hear that, my bro.'

Jonathan sighs and says, 'Thank you, man. Life.'

But because his friend has opened up to him in such a way, David feels that perhaps he should give something in return. That maybe he *could* give something in return. After a few moments he says, 'I can't lie, I've been going through it.'

'Yeah? What's been going on?' says Jonathan.

He pushes down the nightmare. 'Work, init, these people want to finish me,' says David. It's not a lie, more a half-truth. He speaks about the weight of the continual code-switching and the workplace banter which has been taking a toll, albeit virtual. Of colleagues making inappropriate comments and wishing he had said something. 'I'm tired, man,' David says.

'Nah, it's exhausting. Like I said, this country wants us dead.'

'Honestly,' says David and they both share a laugh.

'But for real, think about coming with us to Ghana. This year has been a madness,' says Jonathan.

'I'll let you know, yeah?'

'Alright, cool,' says Jonathan, though he wants to say something more. He pauses. 'I'm always here if you wanna talk, yeah?' And then it comes. 'I love you, bro.'

David feels the same way, but he can't say it. The 'I' is swallowed by something that feels like a lump in his throat, the 'you' also lost. Instead, 'Love bro' falls out of his mouth.

The call ends.

David feels light-headed. He stands up and walks to the balcony. Once again, he looks out to the water. He is not sure what being stuck in London over Christmas for the first time in years will do to him. His eyes fix on the string of lights beneath him for the second time. He looks again at the unlit bulb. He thinks of what it would mean to book a

flight to the land he was so violently snatched from a lifetime ago. Of the demons he may encounter. Of having to
see his mother. He tells himself he can firm it. He knows
that drinking Hennessy with apple juice in the sun with
rounds of tequila shots is the antidote he needs.

He walks back into his apartment and picks up his phone.
In the group chat with the guys he types: *What are the flights
saying?*

Blue lights shine over lounge sofas and shisha stations
surrounded by white-and-blue square decking. Tables
are topped with champagne bottles in iced coolers. Trays
of chicken wings, yam chips and sides of shito abound.
The music is loud, the air is alive with the sounds of afrobeats, the bass of the sound system pulsing through the
venue.

David and Jonathan walk through Bloom Bar, hours after
arriving at the airport and making a quick stop at their
hotel to shower and change. Walking towards the VIP
booth, they are greeted by Emmanuel, who is dressed in
similar attire to them – a pink satin shirt and dark jeans.

'Welcome to Accra, my Gs,' says Emmanuel, standing
up, shouting over the music. He embraces Jonathan and
then David.

'Yes, my guy,' says David, detaching himself from
Emmanuel. 'Is this how you're living? VIP tables, yeah?'

34

'I'm just tryna be like you,' says Emmanuel, and he directs his friends to a booth with a bottle of Cîroc in the middle of the table. He introduces David and Jonathan to a group of men with different accents and pours them all a glass. He holds up his drink, raises a toast and says, 'Bun the UK.'

There is laughter, followed by the clinking of plastic glasses, touching of watches and acrylic nails by a group of women invited to the table.

'Bun the UK,' shouts David in response, 'bun the UK for real.'

Like old times, David is dancing, arms stretched out wide. He sways from side to side, feeling the music in his soul. Periodically, he gathers both Jonathan and Emmanuel, who maintain a chilled demeanour as they raise their red plastic cups into the frame. Together, they dance with women who balance glasses and handheld electric fans. In a call and response, they bellow '*I CAN'T COME AND KILL MYSELF*' into their front-facing cameras, documenting the scene for stories on socials. The vibe is A1. David is back with his boys. He is back in his element. The darkness seems a distant memory.

Shortly after 3 a.m., David steps outside for some air. He finds a bench and takes out his phone to review the story he has posted to Instagram. He is making his way through the comments from followers when a voice catches him off guard.

'Akuetteh?'

David turns around at the sound of his first name. The name for the younger brother. The name that in England teachers struggled to pronounce correctly until eventually he insisted on being referred to by his second name. The name he put on as a mask. But before he was David, he was Akuetteh. Akuetteh from Ghana.

'Akuetteh. You dey Ghana?' repeats the man walking towards him. 'Chale!' he says, taking off the sunglasses he wears despite the darkness of the night.

David's body stiffens. He hasn't seen his younger cousin since he was twelve, only weeks after the accident. When their right hands meet, shoulders drawn in to form an embrace, followed by their middle fingers snapping, David is reminded of the nightmare once more. Of the darkness that overcame him hours ago whilst driving through Accra in Jonathan's rented car. He remembers again the guilt that consumed him passing scenes he did not recognise under the night sky: the horizon lined with towering new buildings, bars and restaurants; G-Wagons and Range Rovers in abundance. He remembers now as he did then that he is here and his brother is not. 'Kwaku,' he hears himself say.

'Chale! How far now? You dey look the same, fresh boy,' says Kwaku, parting from the hug. He gently slaps David's

head, admiring his fresh trim and short twists.
me say you dey come?'

'Sorry, I was gonna WhatsApp you,' says David, though
he wasn't sure what he would have said in the message even
if this were true. He hasn't yet even messaged his mother,
who he hasn't seen in the flesh for nearly three years.

'Nah, chale. I shock o! It's been too long!' There is sadness
in his eyes.

'Yeah, it's good to see you,' says David, lying. The darkness is now spilling out. The nightmare, vivid, though he is
not asleep: blood and broken bones. And the events of that
awful day sweep over him: the scream that escaped him
when he realised his brother was dead. The wail of his
mother at the hospital when she saw the body wrapped in
white linen. His father standing motionless by her side, his
spirit departing his body, never to be the same – vacant.

'Chale, you've come back. You dey feel some way or
nah?'

Fifteen years ago, despite losing half of himself there,
David had begged to stay in Ghana. He didn't want to leave
everything he knew, everything he loved. But his mother
had insisted that the family still proceed with their plans of
relocating to England. Days after his brother's funeral,
she'd said that as a mother she had a duty to give her children a better future, even if there was just one now. Then
he had arrived in a land where he felt the cold in his bones.
A land in which white and Caribbean kids alike laughed at

his accent and asked if he lived in a hut. David steps back, his feet unsteady. 'Sorry, I need some water,' he says, walking away.

Before Kwaku has a chance to respond, his cousin has already disappeared back into the club.

David is drowning. The memories overwhelm him. He wades through the crowd, making his way to the VIP booth. He takes a shot and then another. He downs a glass of rum followed by vodka. But it does not help. The memories are too much, too painful. Maybe it's something about being in the land of his birth. Of being back in the land where his brother lies buried in the ground. He stands up and makes his way to the dance floor to find his boys, ready to go to the next club.

But then there is a spill of alcohol. Disaronno and Coke on fresh white Air Forces.

'Watch the fuck where you're going,' says David, anger washing over him.

'Yoo chill, bro,' says a man whose accent is identical to David's, thick with South London.

It is the word that carries so much weight. The anger is deeper now, laced with guilt.

And then a glass knocked out of a hand and a voice laden with rage carrying over the music, 'I'm not your fucking bro.'

Jonathan and Emmanuel turn around at the sound of their friend's voice. Both experience a déjà vu of sorts. 'D, wagwan?' says Jonathan, walking to David, who is now squaring up to the drink-spiller.

An exchange of words. 'Your boy's moving mad. It's a club for fuck's sake, it's not that deep. You wanna square up?'

A word from Jonathan. 'Come on, D, it's not worth it, let's go, man.' Then an ushering of his friend towards their table. 'Chill.'

'Don't tell me to chill,' David says.

'David, man, let's not do this again,' says Jonathan, his hand now on David's shoulder.

'Get the fuck off me,' says David, shaking off Jonathan's hand. 'And don't tell me to calm down.'

Jonathan takes a step back and turns to Emmanuel. 'Nah, Eman, chat to your boy,' he says.

'Chat to me? You're a big man, chat to me yourself,' says David, edging towards Jonathan.

David and Jonathan stand face to face. A spread of rage. Clenched fists and a tightened jaw. Beads of sweat on temples. To an onlooker, strangers and not two men who have shared nearly a decade of friendship.

Jonathan steps back. 'We're leaving,' he says, turning to Emmanuel. He walks past David and says, 'You can make your own way back to the hotel.'

The crowd that had formed dissipates and the red haze that had overtaken David evaporates. The music is still loud. Ghanaian drill is pumping through every fibre of his body. Suddenly he doesn't know what to do. He makes his way to the bar and takes a seat. And again he sees the man who was the last person to see him cry.

'Chale, come come,' says Kwaku. 'Let me take you home.'

The journey is quiet, with no words shared between them. On the other side of the passenger window there is laughter from men gathered on the roadside. Meat kebabs are being grilled on a makeshift barbecue and night workers board dilapidated tro-tros. Fire and fumes disperse into the night sky.

David and Kwaku arrive at a white house with a red corrugated roof and a large driveway. David steps out of the car. Again, the nightmare comes to mind. He knocks on the door. A light is switched on upstairs. There are foot-steps. A man comes to the door, confusion plastered to his face. Then there is a faint mutter from a woman behind. She is dressed in a red kaftan, her cornrows wrapped under a multicoloured scarf. 'Kofi, who is it?'

He is startled for some time. 'It's Akuetteh.'

She pushes past the man at the door. 'Akuetteh?'

'Mum,' says David.

Before him is the woman he has not seen in years. The woman who represents all he is trying to forget. A reminder of their loss – from a family of four, to three, and then to just two. 'Akuetteh,' she repeats, tears in her eyes.

David steps towards her. The years of hardship come to mind. The years of seeing her work two jobs and taking on extra shifts after his dad died, burdened with debt and no savings. His vow to never again be in such a tight spot, birthing in him a hunger for stability. The reason for him studying economics at university, desperate to secure an investment banking graduate job. But now all of that melts away.

She takes hold of him and says, '*Me ba. Akwaaba.* You're home.'

Inside, his mother scurries around the kitchen, eager to fix him some food despite it being the early hours of the morning. David has a brief conversation with his stepfather, Kofi. They discuss the weather and the approaches to lockdown in the UK and Ghana. Though it has been some years, David is on edge. His mother's second marriage seemed to him an act of betrayal, despite his resentment towards his dead father.

David's mother enters the front room with a plate of crescent-shaped pastries and a mug of Milo. She places it on a small glass table in front of him. 'Meat pie, your favourite,' she says before settling on the sofa next to Kofi. David notices that his stepfather places a hand on his mother's left knee. She looks happy. At ease. For years David had made the excuse of exams and internships, and then the demands of his work, for not joining his mother on her trips back to Ghana. He feels guilty now for refusing to come to her wedding a few months after she moved back permanently.

Suddenly he is aware that he needs the toilet. David stands up and out of politeness says, 'Please, where is the toilet?' though he knows exactly where it is. He walks through the hallway, making his way to the bathroom, passing wooden carvings, plastic-covered Bible scriptures and a church-branded calendar.

He walks up the stairs. On the wall is a framed picture of his graduation. His girlfriend at the time made them do a photo shoot after the ceremony. She posted a picture on Facebook and captioned it *couple goals*, but months later deleted it. He thinks of his mother on that day. Despite the smiles, a sorrow remained in her eyes, and he had been laden with guilt that he was the one to survive and graduate. Afterwards, he'd felt off balance, burying himself in his banking internship and ghosting his girlfriend for weeks. He now thinks of her endless calls and texts, her eventual absence. And his transformation into something else – a Shiny-Suit, Twitter Fuckboy, gaining a reputation amongst girls in the Russell-Group-uni-graduate-job-contingent.

David walks up a few more stairs and sees another picture. It is his mother, his deceased father, his cousin Kwaku and him, twice. He is standing next to his twin brother. They are at the beach they visited often as a family. It was where the trio – Oko, Kwaku and him – would race along the sand and dissolve into laughter whilst eating FanIce sachets. They had been on their way there when the accident happened.

In the morning, David wakes to rays of sunshine streaming through linen curtains, drenching him in light. There are the smells of Hausa koko and kose. He has not had this breakfast since his childhood. He is filled with warmth, and thinks he will extend his stay to be with his mother. To make up for lost time. And then it occurs to him that he has not been visited by the nightmare. He has not woken filled with dread. Instead, he dreamt of the beach. Of waves and white sand. He saw his brother. His body, brown and beautiful. He was surrounded by intricate sandcastles.

He picks up his phone. There is a message from Jonathan, sent hours ago. *Where you at?*

I'm at my mum's house, he types. He continues, *Sorry about last night. Are you free to meet up?*

Jonathan texts back immediately, and David sends him a location.

For the first time in years, David sees Accra in daylight. Sat in an Uber, his eyes take in a place that hasn't been part of his world since he moved to England. He watches as women with multicoloured wrappers swaddled around their waists and babies tied to their backs, weave between vehicles at the traffic lights, selling salted plantain chips, roasted groundnut, face masks, string sponges and packets of chewing gum. On the pavement, food sellers dish out indomie, red stew, waakye and boiled eggs to a queue of customers with empty Tupperware containers in hand. Entering Osu, he sees shop-fronts labelled GOD'S LOVE WOODWORKS and GOD IS GREAT BEAUTY SALON, before passing a wooden shack labelled AUGUSTINA CHOP BAR, where a group of older men dip their hands in a bowl of water, ready to devour a plate of banku and grilled tilapia garnished with onions and tomatoes. The smells of petrol, body odour and roasted corn fill the air. There are the sounds of general chatter, car horns and the shouts of a preacher on an outside speaker. The cacophony of senses triggers an intense feeling, like being reunited with something once lost. He has missed being here. It is home.

An hour later, David's Uber arrives at one of the newer beach houses in Kokrobite. Jonathan emerges from his car minutes later. They greet each other with a nod, the words between them sparse. Side by side they walk in silence towards the beach, where the sun is beginning its descent into the ocean.

'I'm sorry about yesterday, bro. There's no excuse,' says David.

Jonathan does not fill the silence.

David continues. 'Sometimes I get so angry, I can't control it.'

Jonathan softens. 'You need to pattern that, honestly.'

'I know,' says David. He stops. 'I appreciate you man, honestly.'

'I've got you, bro,' said Jonathan.

They pass a donkey with the misspelled words LIVE IT TO GOD imprinted on its left thigh, shepherded by a man with greying hair and a smile that reveals few front teeth.

'I'm a twin, you know,' says David, breaking the quiet.

Jonathan comes to an abrupt halt. 'What? No way.'

'Yeah. Well, I *was* a twin. His name was Oko. Nii Oko Samson Ansah.'

Jonathan waits for David to continue. He knows that unlike *orphan* or *widow*, there is no word for someone who has lost a sibling, a brother. A twin.

'He died,' David eventually adds. 'A car accident when we were twelve.'

'Wow, I'm so sorry,' says Jonathan, though his words feel inadequate.

'We were on our way here actually, for one last time before our move to London. My dad was driving,' says David. 'They never found the other driver. It was a hit-and-run.'

Jonathan brushes his hand over his face. 'Man, that's hard.'

David picks up a small magnolia seashell from the sand. 'We used to come here as kids a lot. He loved building sandcastles. He would build these really detailed structures and decorate them with shells and shit,' he says with a slight smile. 'He wanted to be an architect. He wanted to build a restaurant close to this beach, actually. It was his dream.'

He turns to the shore, looking at how the sky and water meet, recalling his brother's love for nature. Of how he would run to catch the sunset, intrigued by the interplay of light and shadows. How he had once said that no matter what, the sun would always rise the next day. Though Oko was just twelve, he was wise beyond his years. It was like he had been here before.

David's smile disappears. 'That day in the car, he wanted to sit in the middle. We always used to fight over it,' he says. He stops.

Oko was the more intelligent one, the one everyone liked. The one who David admired so much it bordered on worship. The level-headed one, who balanced him out. David has been off balance ever since. He scratches the nape of his neck and tilts his head backwards. 'I think about that day a lot, how different things would have been if we'd been sitting in different seats.'

At times David wondered if his parents had lost their favourite son. That it was possible they had given him the wrong name at birth. It was Oko who was their beloved.

'Nah, D. You can't think like that,' Jonathan says.

David doesn't respond. He is distracted by a bird picking

at the inside of an abandoned coconut. He saw a similar bird at his brother's funeral. Seven days of weeping, but it was never enough to fill the weight of the biggest regret of his life.

'What happened … it's not your fault,' says Jonathan, placing his hand on David's shoulder.

Tears well in David's eyes. He breathes deeply and kneels in the sand. He picks up a handful of grains and allows them to trail through his fingers.

Jonathan squeezes David's shoulder and kneels beside him. And then, for the first time in fifteen years, David weeps. Each tear a severing of anger and regret, the start of a freedom from the pain and guilt that have burdened him for so long. He cries like he did the day he lost half of himself. The better half. His brother and his best friend.

FOR SUCH A TIME AS THIS

You switch on the news. You feel a pain that overwhelms you. Perhaps it is a reminder of your aunt who works night shifts, or her husband who continues to go into work to protect a now vacant building; day in, day out, fearful of the pathogen that has changed everything. Your friend's younger sister, who has sickle cell, who at any time could have a crisis. But it's more than that. They are speaking about you. You, also, could die. Will die.

You reach for your phone and you text the group chat of work colleagues who have become close friends. The girls you met years ago in the bathroom on the fourth floor. You saw yourself in them and them in you. You bonded over hair, Black literature, *Real Housewives* and the unsustainability of bringing your whole self to work. *Guys, this news has really affected me*, you say. *Niah, I feel you, it's proper shit*, says

Mima. *Black people being four times more likely to die from Covid? We actually cannot catch a break*, says Dami, the third in your trio. You start a group FaceTime. You tell them you want to say something. You say you want to speak about it at work. They agree that you should. They say if anyone is to speak, it should be you.

You open up your work laptop. You send a short email to ask what the Network are doing about this new revelation. You wait. You wait some more. You receive an email an hour later.

I have a free afternoon, let's find a time, types the chair of the Network.

Sure, you type and you press Send. You find a thirty-minute slot in the diary and send an invitation. He accepts.

You make your way through the day despite carrying the burden of this grief. The grief invisible to the naked white eye. It consumes you. You cannot shake it. The meetings continue, with the one-to-ones unending. The pointless discussions about things that do not matter. People are dying. Your people are dying. Death surrounds you and they do not care.

You struggle to focus, your attention is elsewhere. You look at the clock. The clock in the corner of video call meetings, where colleagues make dry jokes and struggle to locate the Unmute button. You are waiting for the time in the afternoon to arrive. It does not come.

Time is moving.

But slowly.

Slowly.

The hour finally comes. It is your time to speak. To unburden your thoughts in a semi-safe space. You speak. He listens. You speak about the impact this news may be having on the thirty-three percent of colleagues in the organisation. The impact on their mental health and well-being. You speak about the disproportionate health and socioeconomic impacts, of higher infection rates – and therefore death rates – compared to other communities. You say this is coupled with a financial strain and highlight the disparities in job losses and reduced working hours on top of existing economic inequalities. You speak about the unequal number of people working on the front lines – nurses, cleaners, security guards. You make it personal: you tell him of your cousin who won't be able to sit his exams in the summer. Of how he's likely to receive underpredicted rather than overpredicted grades from his teachers. You tell him about your friend Jada from university, and how her family were not able to have a nine night following her aunt's death. Of how only four of her ten aunts and uncles were able to attend the funeral, and how she herself had watched the service via live stream from her bedroom. You say that all of this adds to already present stress, anxiety and trauma. You end.

He says, I didn't think of it that way. You give him time to collect his thoughts. He continues. Yeah, you're right. We should be saying something. I'll draft an email.

Thank you, you say.

Before leaving the call he says, Maybe you should take the rest of the afternoon off. Log off early? Go for a walk?

You say you are OK. But you are not. You take his advice. You put in your earphones and walk to your local park, passing pictures of rainbows posted in front windows and inscribed on driveways with coloured chalk. You find a bench by the pond and take a seat. You recite a passage, once a 'golden text' learnt decades ago in Sunday school. *He leads me beside quiet waters, he refreshes my soul.* You close your eyes and take some deep breaths. Inhale. Exhale. Inhale. Exhale . . . You play Kendrick Lamar's 'Alright'. You tell yourself it's OK. If God has you, you're going to be alright. You walk back home. An email comes in an hour later. It is sent to the whole Network, with the senior white Race Advocates copied in.

Subject: BAME and Covid

It's a start.

The weeks go on.

You are invited to speak about the impact of the pandemic on Black and brown communities. You use the statistics. But you speak your truth. You recognise your privilege. You have an office job, a good one, and the ability to work from home. You say that everyone you know has lost someone. They are moved. You make your way around the organisation virtually, giving presentations and speaking at staff stand-ups. On top of your usual duties, you are volunteering your personal time to talk about an important issue. You say that it's your corporate contribution. You think you are making an impact. You think you have been called for such a time as this.

But then weeks later you see it. The video lasting eight minutes and forty-six seconds.

The same length of time as a train journey from Woolwich Arsenal to West Silvertown on the DLR. The time you spend doing your evening facial routine with rose-hip oil and vitamin C serum.

In the morning you go for a run. You run to clear your head. But then you stop. You get as far as the end of the hill entering your neighbouring borough. You see Union Jack flags in the windows of three houses in a row. You tell yourself that they are still up from VE Day celebrations, but you aren't sure. There is a banner with the words LET'S MAKE BRITAIN GREAT AGAIN in the front porch of the third house. You start running again. Then you come to a complete standstill. You think of a different fate for yourself whilst jogging. A modern-day lynching with no tree in sight. You remember that he was a similar age to you. You walk back home. You cry when you open the front door.

In the shower your salt tears mix with the water that flows from the showerhead, merging into one, like an ocean. You cry at the thought of eight gunshots and spit, both leading to death. You cry at the knee on a human being's neck as they call out for their mother. You cry at the supposed verdict that saliva from a man with the virus did not lead to the death of a railway worker – a mother, a sister, a human being. You cry at these memories, though not your own, your mind full of tangled images of Black bodies, the Angel of Death as a virus, and the sound of clapping on a Thursday night. You collapse in a heap on the bathroom floor.

You are hurting.

Then you are angry.

You cry out: Lord, don't you care that we are dying? Where are you to pull us out of this storm? Why are you fucking sleeping?

Then you feel as if you are floating. You can't concentrate at work. It's the same sensation you felt the morning after twenty-four storeys of cladding blazed alight. You are there in the office, on the video call, but your mind is elsewhere. You think of how on that Thursday morning a colleague had said, Ah, it's really sad what happened with that tower block. And someone else added, I know, so sad, I heard it's still on fire. And how they then went about their business, getting their morning fix of caffeine in the staff kitchen and discussing their plans for the weekend: a cycle through Burgess Park with the partner and kids, lunch at the pub with old uni mates, and who was getting the drinks for Fizz on Thursday again?

You have a team meeting. You and your manager are the first to join the video call. It is just you and her. To drown out the silence she says, Is that a new hairstyle I see, Niah? She mentions that a colleague from HR has hair just like yours. You could be sisters, she says. No, it's a wig and I'm not mixed-race with braids, are the words you want to say. Instead, you respond with an exhausted smile. But she keeps going. It's so wonderful what you all can do with your hair. I wish I had hair like yours, she confesses, leaning closer into her laptop as if to stroke your frontal closure. She is relentless. I do love all your headwraps though, so exotic in colour, she says. You must wear them when we come back to the office. Are they colours from your country of origin? Nigeria, isn't it? Before you have a chance to respond and say you're actually Caribbean, from Grenada and Jamaica, another colleague joins the call. He says, Sorry I'm late. Childcare.

You feel as if you are drifting in a parallel universe as your colleagues discuss the intricacies of their weekend. A socially distanced catch-up in Peckham Rye Common with the kids and their school friends, a Zoom call with the dreaded mother-in-law. You wait for someone to mention it.

More people join the call, including your colleague's lime-green budgie, who is now part of the team. You should have seen the email, she reminds everyone. The social updates continue. Someone is horrified that his cat walked in on his previous video call. Another laments the pain of not being able to cycle into the office from Brixton Village, picking up an organic chai latte with oat milk on his way into the building.

God, it's so awful what happened, someone says.

The floating ceases momentarily.

I heard the director's dog got put down.

There is a collective sigh at the tragedy. No one mentions it. Everyone states their priorities for the week. The call ends.

You send an iMessage to your girls' group chat. You say, *Guys, I'm really struggling at work today. It's too much.*

Dami responds. *Having people ask how my weekend was, but inside feeling so shit, has been hard.*

Mima replies a few minutes later. *I totally get what you mean. I know I need to be presenting myself in the best way for this new role. But I am exhausted. Honestly, I just want to sleep.*

You start a group FaceTime.

They feel it too. The floating. Black people across the diaspora feel it. The souls of your ancestors buried beneath the tarmac of the streets of Minneapolis feel it. You are tired. You are tired of being tired. This is not the 2020 the God-appointed prophets and apostles of Twitter had declared this decade to be. This was supposed to be the year of blessings and prosperity. For you and your girls it was supposed to be the year of catching flights and living your best lives. It was supposed to be the year of day parties and Afro Nation Part Two. It's a disaster, you say. It's a fucking disaster.

You end the call. You email the Network chair. You say you want to speak again. So you do, this time in writing. You write a blog. One thousand words long. 'Black Lives Matter and What It Means for You.' It is published on your staff intranet. The responses come flooding in. It's the most-liked blog in the history of the organisation. There are endless comments from people across the business, from those at the very top. That was powerful, they say. Black people, Black women across the organisation say they are seen. They are moved to tears. The emails in your inbox say *thank you, thank you for using your voice to convey something I was feeling but couldn't say.* Emotions swamp you. You are invited to speak about systemic racism in the organisation by those in positions of authority. You accept. This is history in the making.

Your girls say, Wow sis, that was amazing. And it is. You are proud that you have used your voice for such a time as this. But you feel overwhelmed. It has been a long week. You are tired. Exhausted from responding to emails from colleagues who ask what they can do to be an ally or how they can teach their children not to be racist. Exhausted from your timeline which is inundated with comments from old school friends asking, *Is it not racist to say that? Surely all lives matter, no?* Exhausted as the memories resurface, the ones buried deep within. Memories of a girl in nursery turning your hand around and asking you why your palms weren't black like the rest of your hand. Memories of being five years old and your mum taking flowers to Stephen Lawrence's memorial plaque, minutes from your house, and telling you he was killed because he was Black. Memories of your dad driving you to your best friend Sharna's sixteenth birthday party and being stopped by the police, who searched his car for the weed he did not have. Memories of being asked by the porter outside Magdalen College where you had got your Oxford University student ID card from, even though you were a postgraduate student.

Mima and Dami tell you that you need a break. They say you have days of annual leave you haven't used yet. You need to look after yourself, they say. You do as they say. You take a week off.

It's the first time you have had a day off work since March. The sun is shining. It is summer. You escape to the garden. You try to video call Sharna, but she doesn't pick up. So you catch up with a church service online. Then you escape into a story. A fictional world where Black people aren't killed because of the colour of their skin.

You breathe. You feel guilty at the breath in your lungs.

You log back into work a week later, where the emails continue to fill your inbox. You make your way through. There is one that stands out amongst the hundreds. It reads: *Hi, I'm getting in touch because your name has been put forward for a new diversity and inclusion role. It would be great to have a chat when you're back from leave.*

You email back immediately. You have the chat. She says the topics that you have been speaking about over the past few months are an important priority for the organisation. She says that the budget is still being finalised, but a full-time paid role will be created, dedicated to this new area of work. She says that the directors have agreed that you are the best person to take on this role. She says that in the interim, they would love for you to take on the extra responsibility on top of your current day-to-day role, given the urgency of the work. You feel warm inside. The timing is perfect, considering that the fixed-term contract for your current role is about to come to an end. It is also a more senior position. You spoke, and this is the time. You feel it again, you hear it: you have come into the kingdom for such a time as this.

You message your girls. They say, *Your voice has created a role for you. Your gift has made room for you.* They say, *We are so proud of you, sis.* You send an email to accept the role.

But days later, you begin to worry. You haven't done your usual due diligence. You send an instant message to your new line manager. You say you would like some clarity. You were in the process of applying and interviewing for other roles with similar levels of responsibility, both internally and externally. You ask when the position will be made permanent.

There is a pause.

Then she is typing . . .

She stops.

Then typing again. *Are you sure you want this role and aren't just chasing promotion?*

The question surprises you.

You want clarity on the position. You have bills to pay. You have responsibilities. It is a pandemic.

You feel a faint stirring in your stomach, but you ignore it.

No, no, I am really passionate about the role. It is what I want to do, you say.

Good, I was just checking. I want someone who is dedicated and not just chasing seniority, she says.

You are confused. But you say, *I really cannot wait to start.* You continue, despite the lingering unease. You show enthusiasm. You say, *Is there anything I can read to be better prepared for the role?*

You think you have diverted the situation. But it's simply a pacifier. You should have known from then.

You start working on your extra responsibilities. It is challenging and fast-paced, but you enjoy it. You are shaping a role, an important role, the first of its kind in the history of the organisation, tackling long-standing racial inequities. You are visible, speaking on a regular basis to the decision makers. Your friends and colleagues congratulate you. They say you are creating change, real change. You are a pioneer.

But you still have doubts. You look at the calendar and see that your contract is coming to an end. You ask again, gently, in conversation with your line manager, when you will move over to your full-time, permanent position. You ask over and over. No clarification is given.

It unsettles you. You remember that you agreed to this role with no correspondence from HR. There was no letter of confirmation of start date or salary. Your mother and father have always told you the importance of getting things in writing. The date of termination is coming. It's getting closer and closer.

The paperwork is a mere formality, she says.

You feel an unease. You feel silly for starting this role in good faith. You speak to a past mentor. Your feelings are valid, she reassures you. She offers to reach out to one of her HR contacts to advise you. You feel settled, temporarily, but the clock is ticking. Word gets back to your line manager. She says, You are getting panicked about this, aren't you? You say you are not, and that you simply want some clarification on the process. She does not respond.

A few days later she asks you to detail what you do in the role. To detail what you do in the role you have created from scratch. It sounds to you like a job description. Finally, the process has started. The vacancy goes up on the recruitment website. You start the application.

There is no guarantee that you will get the job you have been doing for several months now. But at the same time, you have seen how these things can be done if they want you. You have witnessed how recruitment panels are not fair and open at all. You have observed how if a colleague wants a candidate in post who is being interviewed, they will get it. You have seen how scores have been inflated. You should get the job. You are more than likely to get the job, you tell yourself. You are doing it. You created it.

You spend the weekend, and the weekend after that, working on your application. You cancel your plans with your girls to concentrate. Restrictions have eased for the summer, but you decide not to host your annual games night with friends. The friends you haven't seen in the flesh in months. You type in the group chat, *Sorry guys, I can't do it any more. I need to work on this application*, you say. *Obviously you're going to get it*, says Mima. *They created the role for you, it's yours*, says Dami.

But you are not confident. You have a feeling things will not go as they should. And so you get senior mentors to review your application. They say it is strong and that you have nothing to worry about. But they suggest areas for improvement and you implement the changes. You are happy with it. It is the best application you have written. You press Submit.

You continue to work and try to think ahead to interview prep. You put in time with mentors to practise. You have nothing to worry about, they say again. You are great. This role was created for you.

But then two weeks later, the email comes in. It is a calendar invite. Your line manager has put time in your diary for an 'Application Sift'.

Unfortunately, you were not sifted for an interview, she says a few moments into the call.

Not sifted for an *interview?* You feel a discomfort in your bowels.

You were right at the top of my Maybes pile, but in the end we had too many Yeses, I'm afraid, she says.

You are silent.

You have lots of potential, she continues, but you're not quite ready for a role at this level.

You don't say a word.

I love working with you and would love to have you stay in the team. I want to help you to the next stage in your career, she says.

But you think of how she has cancelled every one of your development one-to-ones since starting. You think about the comments on your work: critical and uninformative. Comments of style and not substance. The inappropriate jokes come to mind, and the time she told you to take on a meeting and present despite your reservations, throwing you under the bus.

You remain unemotional. You ask to be sent feedback.

I can understand that this must be upsetting news, she says, but we had a large pool of very strong candidates, with a lot more relevant experience than you. As I said, though, I would still love to have you in the team, but not at this level I'm afraid.

Her smile is insincere. The call ends.

You feel a kick to your stomach.

You message the group chat. You say, *Guys, I didn't get an interview.*

WHAT THE FUCK? is typed back in capital letters. *ARE YOU KIDDING ME?*

Dami initiates a group FaceTime.

Nah, this is some bullshit, Mima says. YOU, Dami says, YOU didn't get an interview?

You feel the tears falling. You are crying.

Girl, I'm so sorry. I'm so sorry, says Dami. You didn't deserve this at all.

Mima continues. Nah sis, don't let these people get to you. You were more than capable, she says. You fucking wrote the job description and you didn't get an interview? You did all of that work and this is how they treat you? Nah, man.

They agree that it's an absolute slap in the face. It's some bullshit, they say.

You wipe your tears.

There is a ping on your laptop. An email has come in. The email you requested. You begin to read: *Though I haven't given any feedback to the other candidates . . .*

You read it out loud in its entirety.

You see the lies on the page, the way things have been

twisted. *You're just not quite ready for a role at this level*, she says again. This time typed.

You continue to read the email.

That's bullshit, they say.

You come to the end of the email.

You know that's some bullshit, right?

You are silent.

Girl, says Dami, don't let these people get you down. You are phenomenal.

Mima says, These guys absolutely fucked you over. They tried it with their BS, but they absolutely do not deserve you.

You take in their words of affirmation. The words that have built you up and made you feel strong again. Then you speak. You say that you are going to reply. You say you're going to write an email. You say you're going to use your words. Your parents taught you how to use your voice. Decades of growing up in a house with dinners sat at the table in the Orange Room, with shelves lined with books, where you and your sisters were taught how to read, how to speak. To debate. You will write, you say. You will speak like you always have. You will use your words as a weapon.

You've got this, they tell you. You can do this. They affirm you, tell you that you are brilliant. Never forget it. And we are here for you. We love you, sis. We are already so proud of you, they say.

You end the call.

You open a blank page on Google Docs to draft your response to the email you were sent. You write. You feel safe in your castle. The four walls of your bedroom and not the office. You type with the strength of your parents and grandparents who travelled from the Islands half a century ago to give you a better future. You type whilst being held by the ancestors. In your mind, you say that they have messed with the wrong woman. The wrong Black woman. You say, she doesn't know who you are. She doesn't know what you have done. She does not know of the community that holds you. She does not know you come from a line of strong Black women who don't take shit. She doesn't know you come from a people who were ripped from their homelands but fought back and survived. They thrived.

You write some more. Then you tweet. You say *Our parents and grandparents didn't come to this country for us to be taken fi eddiat.* There are eighty-seven retweets and fourteen quote tweets. *Yasss,* the replies say, an odd Jamaican flag is stirred into the mix, with clapping hands emojis.

Your hands are weak from typing. You take a break. You sip your glass of water. You plan your next steps. You send a message in yet another safe space you have created. A group chat of other Black colleagues who work in the organisation. You type: *Hey guys, if anyone knows any senior project manager roles going, please let me know, I've been f'd over.*

You return to the page and you write. You have finished. You have a first draft, and you share it with mentors and friends for their views.

You walk downstairs. You tell your parents you didn't get an interview. They are shocked and bewildered, angry on your behalf. But they created the role for you, they say. You tell them you know, but it's OK. You say you plan to use your words to respond. You hug your mum. You embrace your dad. Your younger sister says you are a superstar. They say you are brilliant.

Later it is 10 p.m. You realise you have not eaten. You sit on the sofa with your dad, who reads a newspaper. He puts it down and asks you if you are OK. You don't say anything.

Then the tears fall again.

You weep.

You weep in your father's arms. He holds you. After you have finished crying he reminds you that your name is Niah. That it is Swahili for a woman of purpose. Your mum walks in and hugs you again. She says that you have had a long day in the wilderness. She asks if you have eaten. She leaves and returns. She brings you a plate of food. She is an angel. You eat. Your mum tells you that you are loved. Your dad says that he is so proud of you.

You lay down. You sleep. You dream. You dream that you are in a garden of endless trees planted by streams of water. It is bright, but there is no sun. You see hillsides cloaked in vines and rivers flowing with wine. Ahead of you is a being who is clothed in splendour and majesty. He says, Have I not commanded you? Be strong and courageous. Do not be frightened, and do not be dismayed, for I am with you wherever you go. He smiles.

It is the next morning. You awake early, feeling strengthened. You have another read through the email. Your parents are up too, and when you go downstairs they have comments on the email, ideas that will make it stronger. Bulletproof. Your mentors have another read too. They make suggestions. They make comments. It is ready to go. It is ready to be pushed out into the ocean like the waterproof basket that held Moses.

You read through it once more, from beginning to end. You read out loud. You use the voice that has been shaped by the many years of reading passages of scripture and made-up poems at the front of the congregation at church; your years of being in plays and drama productions. You begin: Thank you for the call yesterday. You say that you've had some time to reflect and wanted to provide some thoughts that you hope she will take time to consider, particularly given the importance of the work. You say that whilst you are disappointed with the decision to not progress your application, it has highlighted many concerns. Since being asked to take up this role, there have been a number of challenges which have epitomised the intrinsic issues of the wider organisation. You say that you had hoped to be part of the solution. You don't speak of what you know is the core problem but focus on the process. You speak of the passion you had for the role, and how you had been concerned about the uncertainty of the informal process from the beginning.

You continue. You say that you are surprised at not being offered an interview given that several senior colleagues fully reviewed your application and provided specific and detailed feedback, all of which you took on board. You note that this is an organisation committed to recognising and supporting talented staff. You say that you were offered the opportunity to take on this challenging role after being recommended by the company's principal leadership – a reflection of your ability and commitment.

You comment on how the feedback given to you falls into one of the most common and frustrating examples of poor reasoning received by Black, Asian and Minority Ethnic (BAME) staff (you use their term). You say specific elements of the feedback given were not mentioned in the job advert and therefore, to you, seem to be out of the scope of the essential criteria. You comment on the process from a best-practice perspective. You bullet-point all the things you have delivered since starting the role. You state the many things you have done outside of your remit.

You continue with a list of three: you say that this is personally discouraging, professionally demoralising and institutionally regressive. You continue with your shots: at a time when leading organisations are trying to embed diversity and inclusion policies and practices in more substantive ways (beyond symbolic gestures), this, in your experience, regrettably, does not augur well.

To end, you say thank you for the offer of staying in the team. But given the somewhat unusual circumstance of being offered an 'in-role' position and then not being short-listed for the very role you have been doing, with praise from seniors, you will be handing in your notice and leaving the company.

You copy in every senior leader in the organisation. You press Send and drop the mic. You release the email to the universe backed by the warriors that surround you, the prayers from your grandparents that kept you. The prayers from before you were knit together in your mother's womb.

You breathe.

But then you remember your sickness. The ailments you ignored because you needed to press on to get the extra work done. You realise your mortality. Your body's calling out to you. You need to rest. Your body is screaming *Rest, rest*. You've been here before, so you listen. You say you cannot come and die for these people. You will not continue to fight whilst sick. You turn on your out of office. You email to cancel your meetings. You switch off your laptop. You send a text to say you are not well and are not sure when you'll be back. You don't wait for a response. You switch off your work phone.

The day continues. You rest. You hear from Mima and Dami that you have caused carnage. You have caused panic. Seniors are not happy. They thought they had made it clear. They say that sound judgement has not been exercised. There is mass hysteria. People are talking. They say, if they could have done that to her, then surely they could do the same to me? You feel strong. A warrior. You rejoice. You feel the ancestors rejoice. What you have done will contribute to a change in internal recruitment policies. You feel that you have been called for such a time as this.

You get a call on your personal phone. She says that what has happened to you is wrong. She wants to help. She is leaving to set up a new team in another organisation. She says that she would love for you to come with her, and that you are brilliant and brave. She offers you a permanent role at a more senior level. She says that it's OK if you think about it and focus on getting better. You feel you have won. And you have. You are happy it has happened to you. You have victory. You accept the new role you have been offered.

But then you feel sad.

Then you ghost.

You move from anger, to hurt, to anger again. The reality of what has happened dawns on you. Your parents have told you similar stories about barriers to progression at their places of work. You also think of the stories from your grandparents – no Blacks, no dogs, no Irish, not only at work but in places of worship. You remember that despite being the third generation on this soil, things have not changed, not really.

The days go on. You are tired from battle. You order takeaway even though it is a Tuesday, and do the same again on Thursday. You send a text message to Sharna to say you are going through it. She doesn't get back to you. You spend longer than usual in bed. You are tired. Mentally and emotionally. And you are sick. You are exhausted.

You message the girls. They say to rest, to take all the time you need. They say you have been through a traumatic experience. And so you rest again.

A week later, you log on to tie up loose ends. You feel stronger. Your body has healed. Messages relating to your mic drop email flood your inbox. You know they will want to portray you as the angry Black woman, too emotional. So you keep it professional. You decline offers of speaking on a video call. You say that everything you wanted to say was in that email.

You hear that the woman who has f'ed you over has been signed off from work for stress and anxiety for months. You say that this is the embodiment of white women's tears. She has pulled out the mental health card. The card reserved only for certain segments of society. She is playing the victim. But *you* are the victim. No, you are a survivor. And now you have to be strong.

Maintaining good working relationships has always been important to you, so you send an email to the fifty-seven people you have worked with over the last few months. You say that due to unforeseen circumstances you are no longer in post and have accepted a role that you will be starting soon outside of the organisation. You do not explain why. You do not explain the racism. You do not explain the ageism. You do not explain the intersectionality. The emails trickle in. *I am so sorry to hear that. You were fantastic. I hope everything is OK.*

Then one email comes as a shock. *I have an interview for that role*, it reads, *always happy to chat*. You are stunned. You laugh. Then you are confused. How is it that *he* was offered an interview and you were not?

You message your girls. They can't believe it. *Nah, shut up please*, they say.

You send an email back. *Yes*, he replies, minutes later. He confirms that he has an interview on Monday for the role that should have been yours. Monday at 1.30 p.m. You laugh again. Him? you ask yourself. To your knowledge he doesn't have the very things you were told you don't have. He is at a lower level than you. He is a white man. You are angry. It is worse than you thought, but you should have known.

This is what they do, you remind yourself. They don't care about you. Black lives do not matter. Not now, not ever. Don't believe the hype. Don't believe the black squares. This country is not for us. It is not for you. It never will be. The words of Paul Gilroy come to mind. There ain't no Black in the Union Jack.

You are mad. You send an email to a superior. You say you are shocked at this news, given what you were told about your application. But she says, *As you know, I was not involved in the recruitment process.* You are in awe. So you go higher. You are met with a similar washing of hands. *As you know, I was not involved in the recruitment process,* he repeats. *But I know it was fair and open,* he says.

Bullshit. You are angry again. Anger that is red. Blood red.

Then your anger turns to tears. You cry. You thought this was the time, for such a time as this, but you were wrong.

You call your older sister. You cry on the phone. She says, I know, I know babe. It's OK to cry. Cry, cry, she says. And you do. But babe, she says, you need to try to let this go. You can't let the anger eat you up.

You move on to your new role. You are present but know you are doing the bare minimum compared to your usual high standards. They are impressed by your work. But you are coasting. In your group chat, you tell your girls you don't want to have anything to do with diversity and inclusion at work. You decline the company's many requests to be the independent BAME panel member. You decline requests for Black History Month speaking engagements.

You decline everything. You hand in your Black Excellence card. This is your protest. You say you don't care for it. You say you are done. But you are hurting.

Weeks later, it is a Sunday. During the evening you watch an episode of *Small Axe* on BBC One with your parents and younger sister. It is the story of the Mangrove Nine. Something stirs in you, you can't shift it. Maybe it's the racism that is still present three generations on.

And then later you pray.

You say, Father, remove the anger and the hurt. You say, Lord, give me the strength and the opportunity to forgive them. You pray for your enemies. All of them. All of them who did wrong and should have done what was required.

Then you hear it again. You turn to Esther 4:14. *What if you have come into the kingdom for such a time as this?* And then you write. You pour out your rage, your trauma, not knowing that your pain is turning into art. The words written mixed with tears, the content for a story. And so you write, and you cry, and you write some more. You can feel it. This is the thing, this has always been the thing. You write for such time as this. Maybe this was always the time. Perhaps all of it, every element of it was and is the time. This is the time: for such a time as this.

LOVE IN CRISIS

When Michael suggested meeting up for the second time, my younger sister, Shalom, had just had a crisis.

She said the pain was like nothing she'd ever known. Like having a migraine in every crevice of her body, piercing daggers thrust into her skin and her bones broken over and over. This time, her hands and feet were swollen and she was struggling to breathe. As usual, it had begun suddenly, with relentless pain in her chest, back and legs. As usual, I felt helpless.

'How are you doing, girl?' I asked as I sat at her bedside in the hospital hours later.

'I'm OK,' breathed Shalom, drowsy from the morphine she'd been given.

But I knew she was far from OK. Beyond the physical agony, I knew she was upset she would now be missing her best friend's twenty-first birthday party. I knew she was frustrated about having to convince people of her pain. I knew she was angry, questioning why her.

'You'll be out soon, baby girl. And we can just chill and catch up with *Real Housewives* like we always do,' I said, trying my best to stay optimistic.

She smiled slightly and closed her eyes, which looked bare without her usual lash extensions. 'Did you bring the Twix?' she whispered, not opening her eyes.

'Of course. Twix Xtra, as requested,' I said and put by her side three of the chocolate bars she ate way too many of. I leaned in closer, tucking in her fluffy hot water bottle and readjusting the blanket I had packed in her emergency bag just before the ambulance arrived.

Shalom drifted into sleep and I watched as her chest rose and fell. I thought of how we had nearly lost her a year ago. Of how, when the paramedics entered our front room, we'd said she needed morphine because she was having a crisis but had been met with hesitation. Of how the nurse on duty that day also hadn't heard of her condition. Of how it had taken so much longer for Shalom to get a blood transfusion. Of how she'd then caught Covid and almost died.

As I watched air enter and leave her lungs, I thought of the possibility of her breath one day ceasing. Of the possibility of my baby sister's dreams being cut short. I thought of her love for make-up and desire to become an award-winning MUA. Of her entrepreneurial spirit, wanting to take her cupcake business to the next level. Of her love for children and volunteering in the creche at church. Of how on her best days she was a joy to so many people.

Then I thought of Michael, and his message that I had left on read. I replied. I told him I was busy, without explanation. I lied for a second time, not because of my sister but because I knew what a first date would mean. I wanted to delay it for as long as possible because of what I knew I needed to ask. And I was terrified of what his answer might be.

Weeks before, Michael and I had met in the traditional way – online. With things returning to normal, my girls had told me that now was the time to start dating. After our book club meeting one evening, Niah stayed on the video call and delivered her TED Talk. 'Listen, Dami, you need to go out, out. But you also need to be open to what they call "strategic positioning". You have to post more pictures of yourself on socials.'

I figured it was time. I heeded Niah's advice and also downloaded Hinge, as Mima said the stock had improved over the last few years. Through a combination of messages and voice notes, I had a back and forth with the girls in our group chat about what pictures would be best to upload to my profile.

You want a mix of pictures that show your best angles in good lighting, typed Niah.

And ones that show your personality, messaged Mima soon afterwards. They briefed me on the best conversation starters to add and cautioned me on what to avoid, including men who wanted to know if you could cook and those who said they were looking for their 'Queen'.

After the short masterclass, I updated my profile with more flattering pictures taken during summer months, with fresh braids and my face beat, and added a range of conversation starters to my profile, which the girls approved of.

Days later, Michael commented on a prompt that read *Do you agree or disagree that* . . . Fresh Prince *is the best show of all time?* He said, *Absolute facts.* My Wife and Kids *has nothing on* Fresh Prince.

I scrolled through his profile. He had a nice face and body and seemed to say things of substance. His feed was free from nausea-inducing videos of him bumping weights in the gym, nor was there reference to looking for a woman who possessed feminine energy. Twenty-seven years old. 5'11". London. Moderate political views. After screen-recording his profile and sending it to the girls' group chat, I gave him a like back.

We had only been speaking for a few days when we began sending messages the length of essays. Next came the voice notes, then his suggestion that we should transition to WhatsApp as it offered more variety: replying to individual messages and sending GIFs. Though hesitant, I gave him my number. After all this time, it was nice speaking to someone who was genuinely interested in me, someone who wanted to delve into the particularities of what made me, me. Of having someone who replied to every element of what I had shared, like he had taken notes before responding.

And he interested me too. I was impressed by his ambition, but also his humility. I loved the kindness displayed in his everyday life. Like how he had brunch every Saturday afternoon with his parents and in his spare time mentored a group of students from his old school to help with their university applications.

A week went by, and we moved from late-night phone calls to video calls. The first time we FaceTimed we talked until the early hours about everything: our love for travel and for food, what we did for work, our dreams and aspirations. Though he wasn't a reader, he wanted to hear more about my book club and asked for recommendations based on my all-time favourites. He shared his passion for the outdoors and for climbing, which I hadn't considered as hobbies for myself but was now eager to explore.

I loved that he remembered small details I'd shared with him. After so long, it was refreshing to have someone who checked in first thing to say good morning and asked if my ongoing back pain had prevented me from sleeping through the night. And someone who, before the final interview for my new job, sent a message that afternoon saying that I was absolutely going to smash it. And he always made me laugh. Deep down, I enjoyed being the centre of someone's world again. Then I felt something I hadn't felt in years: I was catching feelings.

I feel like you're putting off meeting up, Michael typed in response to my message. *If you're not on it, it's cool. Just let me know.*

But I was on it. I liked him. I liked him a lot. And I was taken by his thoughtfulness in planning our first date. Of how he sent bullet-point lists with options of the places we could go to, bearing in mind my love for Thai food and factoring in my pescatarian diet. I loved his suggestions for pre-dinner activities: axe throwing, an escape room, or something more chilled, like a rooftop bar for drinks. I really did want to finally see him in person and had far exceeded the ideal time frame of meeting up within two weeks. But I knew what a first date would mean. I knew what I would need to reveal. I didn't want to have to think about the implications of this new-found love. I wasn't ready for the potential heartache.

Years before, I had fallen in love. Olamide and I had met at the back of the 51 bus on our way into college. I thought our love story together would follow the classic blueprint: friends-turned-lovers who would date for nearly a decade and then make it official at twenty-five. We would have multiple holidays a year, making the most of our time alone, before having our first child at twenty-seven and our second at twenty-nine. I thought we would be surrounded by a community of peers who had also married in their twenties, with a village of children raised as family in our thirties. That had been the plan.

But then days before we were both due to leave for university in different parts of the country, he said, 'I think we need to break up, Dami.'

'What do you mean?' I asked, completely and utterly confused. 'We spoke about the long distance. We said we would make it work.'

'I know,' he said.

'So what are you even talking about?'

He didn't say anything for a while and then looked up at me. 'I was speaking to my mum. I told her about our plans of getting married and having a family one day.' He stopped. 'She told me to take a blood test, D.'

Then came the words that ended everything.

Shalom rolled over and turned to face me.

'Hey babes,' I said. 'Are you hungry? What do you fancy?'

'Mmm. Can I get Nando's, please?'

'Of course. Your usual, yeah?'

'Yes, please.'

'Chips or garlic bread? Or both?'

'Both,' she said with a smile.

'Got you,' I said, scrolling to the Deliveroo app.

'Dami,' said Shalom, just as I was double-checking her order.

'Yes, sis,' I said, not looking at her.

'Do you think I would still be here if Mum and Dad had checked before they got married?' she said.

I looked up. 'Shalom, I—' I stopped.

Though I never said it, I thought about it often. After all, it was the reason Ola's mum had said we should break up, saying it was the responsible thing to do. 'One in four' is what Ola told me the day he broke my heart. That the combination of his AS genotype and mine – the same combination as my mum and dad – equated to a one in four chance of our future children being born with sickle cell. Shalom had been the one in the four.

'Babes, I don't know,' I said, and regretted it at once.

'I wish they had checked,' said Shalom, tears in her eyes.

'Hi, Shalom,' said a nurse, walking over to her bedside, interrupting the words I didn't have. 'I'm here to run a few tests.'

As the nurse inserted another IV bag of fluids into Shalom's veins, I turned away, feeling a lump in my throat. 'I'm going to the loo,' I said. 'I'll be back in a sec.'

In the toilet, I shut the door and cried soundless tears into my lap. I wished, like I did from time to time, that I was the one who had unusually shaped red blood cells and not Shalom. I wanted to take on her pain and make it my own. I wished we could trade places. I thought back to my sister aged seven, the day her classmates decided she would be the 'monster' in the game they had made up because of the yellow in her eyes. I thought of how she had been laughed at in secondary school when her complexion changed to a deeper shade of brown, a result of the medication intended to help produce healthy blood cells. I wished it was her and not me who had found an empty packet of skin-lightening cream in the bathroom bin days later. I wanted it to be me who had overheard our parents arguing about her going on a school residential, my mum worried she might have a crisis. And I wanted to take away the pain she felt when she questioned, both aloud and in silence, why she was the only one of our siblings who had been born this way. As I had then, I felt guilty.

I cried some more. I cursed God and then begged for forgiveness. I prayed the prayers my mother taught me. First in English, then in Yoruba. I whispered Psalm 91, with particular emphasis on *A thousand may fall at your side, ten thousand at your right hand, but it will not come near you.* I spoke the verses over my sister. Then I prayed the words over myself, thinking of Michael. The girls always said that on the other side of twenty-five, it was difficult to find a Black man who loved God, who was doing well for himself, and who wasn't an anti-feminist dickhead. I stopped. It was just a date. I was getting ahead of myself thinking about children that might not even materialise. I backtracked and rationalised that twenty-five percent was, in fact, a small percentage. I said that, in any case, I would have the prayers of my mother and her army of Nigerian aunties from the

University of WhatsApp. I would be covered by their hour of prayer and intercession that took place every Tuesday and Thursday at 5 a.m. But then I thought of Shalom constantly in hospital and the pain that consumed her. I thought of bringing a child into the world who might suffer in the way she did. I thought again about how she had nearly died.

After I had cried the tears I didn't know I had left, I picked up my phone. I decided not to wait until the first date. I texted Michael, with no context, unprovoked, the question my parents should have asked each other all those years ago. I said: *Do you know what your genotype is?*

He didn't text me back.

He called me immediately.

SUMMER

Summer. The time of day parties, picnics in the park and late-night drives. Where the sun is shining bright, a balm to the myriad of changes both thrust upon you and the ones chosen. The time of longer evenings and watching the sky blood red, bleeding into night. The time that makes us forget. Makes you forget. But on this late Saturday morning, you again roll over in bed and switch your phone to airplane mode.

David had just caused a flurry of notifications in the university group chat that was still active six years on from your graduation.

Impromptu BBQ, what are you man saying?

Jonathan came in a few moments later and said, *You hosting, yeah?*

Nah, I'll leave that to Eman.

Emmanuel jumped in with his rebuttal and said, *Are you not the one with those balcony views though?*

The girls appeared minutes later and added their twopence, laced in lols and emojis. The conversation went on for almost an hour, with discussions about the best location for the afternoon link-up, who would be making the marinated meats, what side dishes to prepare and who would be bringing the rum punch. You hadn't yet confirmed your attendance. You hadn't said a word, so Niah @ed you and asked, *Sis, are you free?* But you couldn't reply. You didn't have the energy.

The post on Instagram that you wish you hadn't seen the day before had come to mind. The content you had tried your best to avoid. The caption: *Thank you for being my forever person.* The picture: Tolu on one knee, with the sunshine returned to his eyes, rose petals surrounding a woman who wasn't you. Anyone else might have cried, but you're not a crier. You never have been. You rolled over and tried your best to drift back into sleep, even though it was 1 p.m. Even though the sun was shining bright. Even though it was summer. You put the duvet over your head and thought back to when you and Tolu first met.

'That smells ever so exotic, Jada. What is it?'

Everything in you wants to say *Mind your own business, Heather*, but your mother's advice to 'walk good' comes to mind. Your mouth contorts into a fake smile and out come the words, 'It's jollof rice and beef stew.'

'Oh yes, je-llof rice,' says Heather from the food start-up, who also co-works from your shared office space in Shoreditch. You remove your discoloured Tupperware from the microwave. She looks intently at the fire-yellow rice, layered with generous pieces of meat coated in brown sauce. Her nose moves towards the takeaway container from your friend's party the night before, all notions of personal space vanishing. Her eyes light up. 'It smells ever so spicy. Is it like paella?'

You close the microwave door. 'Erm, not really,' you say, trying to mask your irritation.

'Sho-la brought in something similar a few weeks ago. So authentically African,' she says, before putting her pesto mixed-grain quinoa and grilled salmon into the microwave.

'I'm sure,' you say.

You are desperate to get out of the kitchen. But you need to wash the bowl you used earlier this morning for break-fast. You feel her eyes on you.

'You do know you don't need to bring in your own sponge, right? Everything in the kitchen is communal,' she says.

You do know. It's the reason you brought in your own. Ever since you saw someone wipe their neck with the sponge provided at the sink, you started bringing your own from home without fail. You were on the receiving end of continual questions, namely: 'Why is the sponge in an ice-cream container, Jada?' But you continued anyway and responded when you could be bothered, using the same repurposed line: 'I just prefer to use my own things. And it's good for the environment – reduce, reuse, all that good stuff.'

There is a laugh. You leave the kitchen. You take a few steps forward, and that's where you see him. The first thing you notice is the sunshine in his eyes. 'You dealt with that well,' he says. He has taken the casual dress code to a whole new level and wears a navy Adidas tracksuit and Jordans. Seeing him first reminds you of your brother and then of your cousins.

'Mate. It all gets so exhausting. I just wanted to eat sha,' you say.

He laughs. 'I feel you. You heading over there?' he says and points to the communal area to your right.

'Yes,' you say, lying. You had planned to go to the uninhabited area of the building and escape for nearly an hour to watch an episode of *Insecure*. But you are taken by the sunshine in his eyes.

And that's how you met. Love found on a heated plate of microaggressions, stirred together by Heather in the staff kitchen. Years afterwards, you would both refer to it as Jollofgate, grateful the moment had brought you together. But you haven't eaten your favourite dish in months.

*

There is a knock on your bedroom door. 'Jada,' says a firm voice.

You are in a daze. 'Mum,' you manage. 'I'm sleeping.'

'Your friends are here.'

You sit upright. 'What? How?'

Your mum enters your room. 'Should I tell them they can come up?'

You hesitate but eventually respond, 'Yeah, sure.'

You turn to the mirror, wiping the sleep from your eyes. Though it is nearly 3 p.m., you haven't yet showered. Though it is a Saturday. You haven't been outside in days, though the sun is shining bright. Though it is summer.

You hear the voice of your best friend as she walks up the stairs. You smile. This is so like her to do this. To turn up unannounced when she has not heard from you, ghosting for days. For the times when your grief is bottomless, with waves crashing into you, overwhelming your very depths. For the times where you can no longer see the sun, though it shines bright. Though it is summer.

'Guys, man,' you say as Destiny, along with Niah, Gabby, Sharna and Rianna, enters your room. They each lean over to hug you. You see a bag in Destiny's hands.

Over the years, she has turned up with endless gifts and words of encouragement. When your aunt died, after the cancer came again for her left breast, she sent you a mango-scented candle with the words IN LOVING MEMORY OF AUNTY JACKIE. When you were made redundant, she suggested a walk and bought you pizza to eat together on a park bench. You are grateful for all the times she has sent you links to gospel songs and has called to pray for you though you are more agnostic than a believer. For the times she gifted you with a book about Black joy during the month of June, when your heart was breaking. She is the most thoughtful person you know.

'For you, babes,' Destiny says as she hands you the bag. Inside is a bunch of yellow roses, an extra-large bar of Cadbury Dairy Milk and a bag of Thai Sweet Chilli Sensations crisps.

'Why are you guys actually like this?' you say.

'Big up, Destiny man,' says Niah. 'She rallied the troops.'

'I appreciate you,' you say. You figure that after airing Destiny's messages and the messages in the group chats, she would have realised something was up. You know now, after all the years that have passed since you met at university, that she would have set up a secret group chat and assembled your closest of friends – Niah and Sharna, whom you also met in first year, and Gabby and Rianna, whom you met at one of Niah's games nights on the cusp of turning twenty. You know Destiny would have said that they needed you. That you needed your Avengers. And now they are here.

'No worries, sis,' Destiny says as she settles in a chair in the corner of your room. Niah and Gabby find a seat on your bed. Rianna and Sharna sit on the floor.

'How are you doing, girl?' asks Gabby.

'Meh, I've been better,' you say.

'I hear that,' Gabby replies after an exhausted sigh. You know she can relate to experiencing a loss, though there isn't a body in the ground. That heartache never quite leaves you.

'We saw his post,' says Niah. 'I'm so sorry.'

Again if you were a crier, you might have cried. But that's not you. You don't cry during sad movies. You didn't cry when you watched your aunt's body being lowered into the ground. You don't cry, but you hold things deep within. It's the place where you still hold him.

Words are stuck in your throat. What you want to ask is *How did he get over me so quickly?* You want to ask *Was what we had even real?* Finally you say, 'How did he find someone so soon?'

Your girls are speaking, but you don't hear their words.

You think back to months after Jollofgate, when you moved in together. Your parents thought it was premature. But you said, 'When you know, you know.' You enjoyed playing house. Him folding clothes on a Saturday morning whilst you made your dad's signature eggs with a drop of honey and a dash of seasoned salt. You introduced him to Kehinde Wiley and coconut milk and he shared his love for anime and tried to explain the offside rule to you. You spoke often about the diversity of contemporary African and Caribbean art and your dream of curating an exhibition, and he schooled you on cryptocurrency and the intricacies of his trading business. You discovered each other's annoying habits – you leaving the lights on for vibes and him not wanting to throw away disposable glass dessert containers. On your two-year anniversary, days before lockdown, he proposed. Weeks after, when you were admiring the silver princess-cut diamond ring on your left hand, he told you that he had originally planned a getaway to Italy. That he had wanted to ask the question overlooking the Colosseum. In the end he'd had to cancel and had his friends help decorate the flat he owned but which you had made your home. Despite it being plan B, it was the still happiest day of your life.

You zone back in. 'Don't mind Tolu anyway. He's short,' says Sharna.

'Sharna, man. Don't be so shallow,' says Destiny.

'Is she lying though?' says Niah.

'No lies were told,' says Rianna.

They burst into laughter. You do too. But it's the thing you admired about him. He was not a man of height but he had such a large presence. Everyone knew when he entered a room. You felt safe with him. You felt at home. Until you didn't.

'But girl, honestly. You're doing so well,' says Destiny, interrupting your thoughts.

At first you were both happy about spending so much time together. More time to bask in each other's company, more time to Netflix and chill. You made the most of being at home and ordered a wedding planner notebook and started to make plans for the big day. You discussed the colour scheme and the decorations. You imagined how Jamaica would meet Nigeria. How you would bring together the island's national dress with ankara, and the meeting of brown stew chicken and egusi soup at the reception. You discussed your extended honeymoon and your plans to travel first to the Caribbean and then to West Africa. You even discussed baby names. But in the end there were only so many series you could binge-watch. There were only so many afternoon and evening walks you could go on.

'Yeah girl. We're so proud of you,' says Niah.

You manage a smile.

You picture the woman surrounded by rose petals. Though you don't know her, you imagine Tolu's new fiancée to be a Corporate Babe, most likely in finance. You think maybe she is fully Nigerian and not just half like you. You wonder if she has a thriving side hustle and is on track to buy her second property.

You open the packet of crisps and pass them round. 'I actually don't know what I have done with my life,' you say.

'Girl, please,' says Rianna. 'You're killing it.'

'Also some grace please. The pandemic has really fucked us all over,' says Gabby.

You take in their words. But though he never said it, you often felt that the sunshine in Tolu's eyes was dimming because of you. You thought maybe you were too mediocre for the force he was – the founder of a new tech company, with a passion for increasing financial literacy. You're not sure what shifted in you both, but being alone together so much provided the perfect conditions for you to drift apart. How the differences between you started to eclipse your affection and the interests you realised were not so common at all. In the end it was mutual. You both said it was over without saying the words explicitly. You are triggered every time you see wedding posts on socials. You were supposed to be the first of your friends to walk down the aisle. You still carry the shame of being once engaged and now single.

'Before lockdown, I would have never imagined I'd be back here, back in my parents' house,' you say.

'I hear it, babes. But it's OK. Don't put too much pressure on yourself,' says Destiny, taking a handful of crisps.

'For real. Our plans change, and that's OK,' says Rianna.

So much of your life was bound up with Tolu. You had made a bucket list. You were supposed to travel together, ticking off the Seven Wonders of the World, both new and ancient. You spoke of a week-long safari in Masai Mara and cycle tours with Table Mountain and Frenchman's Cove in view. You discussed remote working from Bali for six months and road trips through Central Europe.

'Come on girl, your future is still so, so bright,' says Niah.

'Orange,' says Destiny.

'And be kind to yourself, babe. This heartache thing, it takes time even if you decide to end it. Trust me, I know,' says Gabby.

Again you think of the woman surrounded by rose petals. You don't know how they met, but you made up a scenario. Shortly after you moved out, he went out even more to drown his sorrows. He met a woman at a club and had a one-night stand, and weeks later she discovered she was pregnant. He wanted to do things the traditional way and suggested they get married. You didn't believe he could have found such a genuine connection in someone he had just met.

'You're gonna be OK. It gets easier,' Gabby continues, squeezing your hand.

There are collective nods and smiles. You smile too.

This is what you do. You and your closest friends support each other in the good times and in the bad. When Gabby bought her flat, you gathered with Prosecco to celebrate, and did the same when Sharna qualified as an associate lawyer. You were all there for the launch of Rianna's social enterprise to promote diversity in water sports, and went for a late-night drive when Destiny passed her driving test on her fifth attempt. You remember Niah's words on your first girls' trip to celebrate every milestone – big and small.

Rianna's phone vibrates. She picks it up. 'Nah guys, this app is not for me. I've decided,' she says.

'Ri, you say this every month,' says Niah.

'I know, but this time I mean it. Look at this please?' says Rianna and passes her phone to Destiny. 'Did this man really just say, "I hope you know CPR because you are taking my breath away"?'

'Stop it,' Gabby groans.

'I cannot with the cringe,' you say.

'God, get us out of the ghetto,' adds Sharna.

Again there is laughter. You are grateful that you are together like this in your room. You have missed these moments. You have missed the times when you would chill in your room after Youth Service at church, your aim to 'look for man', as Rianna would say, instead of deepening your relationship with the Lord. You have missed the times they have slept over and you have watched hours of *Girlfriends* together, staying up till the early hours in stitches of laughter about anything and everything.

'I'm deleting this dating app,' says Rianna.

You all laugh, knowing she will most likely download it again next week.

'So this barbecue you guys were talking about,' says Rianna.

'I'm down. I mean, it has been a minute,' says Niah.

'What do you say, babe?' says Destiny, facing you.

'I dunno. I'm not really in the mood,' you say.

'I think it will be good for you,' says Rianna.

'Maybe,' you say.

'Did you ever get rid of his stuff in the end?' asks Destiny.

'I didn't.' Everything is still in your cupboard. Years of memories in a transparent box that is preventing the door from closing.

'You should throw it out. Burn some stuff too,' says Sharna.

'Agreed. We should do it now,' says Gabby, standing up.

'Now?' you say.

'Yup, do it,' says Rianna.

You think that maybe out of death will come something new. Life. New hope. You think that perhaps this is the sacrifice that needs to be made. That on the other side of the fire is salvation. You get out of bed. You open the cupboard door and sigh. You see the transparent box.

'Burn it all, girl,' says Rianna.

The sentimentalist in you is hesitant. But the girls say it is time.

'Burning is dramatic but necessary,' says Destiny. 'A symbol.'

You think about all these things and then you say, 'OK, let's do it.'

The girls cheer.

Minutes later, you return from the kitchen with opaque black bags. You fill them with old hoodies and teddy bears, trinkets received from Valentine's Days and birthdays over the years. The girls help you divide other items into two piles – one for the charity shop and another to be picked up by the refuse collectors. It is nearly six when you are all outside in the garden. You pass around a plate of sliced hardo bread and glasses of Ribena like it is Easter weekend. Niah adds fuel to a makeshift barbecue. Rianna places into your hands things that can be burnt – pictures, letters and cards.

'You've got this,' says Destiny. Gabby places a gentle hand on your back.

You step forward. You give to the red-orange flames all the memories from your time with him. The memories now overlaid with heartache, no longer the delight they once were. As the fire rages, you take a seat. You sip the Ribena, slightly warmed from the sun, and take a small bite of the sweet-tasting bread. You watch as parts of you are cremated by lighter fuel and flames. You watch as they turn to grey ash.

'This is good, babes. Make room for your blessing,' says Gabby, though what she says is not delivered with much vim. You wonder if she has performed a similar ritual before. You wonder if it helped. She squeezes your hand.

You drain the crimson liquid from your cup and breathe in the fumes from the fire. You bow your head, then look up to the sky.

'Proud of you, girl,' says Destiny. Everyone else smiles.

'So, we've already got this barbecue set up. We may as well call the boys. What do you reckon?' you say.

'Let's do it,' says Rianna.

'I'm gonna head home,' says Gabby. 'I need to finish up some work.'

'On a Saturday?' you say.

'Yeah, girl. You know how it is.'

'I should probably do the same. But I'll stay for a bit,' says Sharna.

Both Niah and Rianna say they are down.

You send a message in your university group chat, then send out a broadcast. The girls do the same.

An hour later, the boys have arrived and the garden is smoky, filled with the fragrance of chicken, lamb ribs, burgers and the charred scent of grilled peppers, onions and corn. Just before midnight, your garden is full of your closest friends and anyone else who was looking for a motive. Then, between sips of Sharna's home-made rum punch, you dance. You let go. You get lit. You sing from your depths the lyrics of your favourite 90s hip-hop song with your girls.

Niah shouts, 'Your future is so bright, girl.'

Destiny, Sharna and Rianna scream in unison, 'Orange!'

REGGIE

Before Grandad told me he was dying, I knew.

A younger, more zealous me would have said it was a prompting from the Holy Spirit. On the phone, amongst his usual eschatological talk, on the evening restrictions were lifted, he said, 'I'm not too wonderful, Sharn, mi belly not good at'al and mi back stiff up'. There was an immediacy to his typical refrain of 'going home to be with the Lawd', something he had been saying for at least the near three decades I had been alive.

And then he revealed the sickness in his lungs that had spread to his liver and kidneys. He said the doctor didn't know how long he had left. I held back the tears I could feel in my throat, though some escaped. I took a seat on my bed to steady myself. He said he would call my mother. I was relieved. I wasn't ready to speak to her, not yet.

Before hanging up, for the first time I told him I loved him.

Rubbing away the tears that had smudged my foundation, I opened my laptop. I had already booked off a week's annual leave, with plans to find a last-minute all-inclusive package. Somewhere remote with sun and sea, where I could forget for a few days the bad decisions I had made over the past few months. Instead, I felt an urgency to change my plans.

I looked into the mirror at the Adinkra Gye Nyame symbol tattooed on my left arm and the black and blonde sisterlocks that flowed beyond my shoulders. These were the supposed markers of rebellion in my adult life that had previously stopped me visiting Grandad, pre-empting his old-school Pentecostal disapproval. But they now paled into insignificance. I needed to see him for the last time.

A week later, Raymond, who has been Grandad's driver ever since he retired and moved back to Jamaica over twenty-five years ago, meets me at the airport. He says, 'What a way yuh have put on weight, Miss Sharna,' and I force a smile. I remember that Caribbean elders have no filter. The air is hot, hotter than I remember, but I am disappointed not to see the sun. It is overcast and looks like it may rain. Outside the airport, the roads are full of cars, trucks and men and women alike, who walk on the roadside with a gentle sway in their hips, lacking any sense of urgency. It is this slow walk, in contrast to my hurried step, that always gives it away. That they are from here and I am not. I am reminded of the words of Ijeoma Umebinyuo: *So, here you are / too foreign for home / too foreign for here / Never enough for both.* 'Diaspora Blues.'

Sat in traffic, I see a red-and-white billboard that reads GET NUFF DATA, MORE TALK and a message from the Ministry of Transport that says PROTECT YOUR HEAD, DON'T END UP DEAD. A man in a black, green and yellow ONE LOVE JAMAICA T-shirt walks between the vehicles shouting, 'Wata, wata, banana, banana,' with bottles of water labelled WATA in hand and bunches of bananas on a plate on his head. 'Smile Jamaica' by Chronixx echoes from a sound system in a truck with a sticker on its bumper stating GOD'S MERCIES, GOD ALONE. The music is loud, but I don't feel rattled.

I have the window open. I smell the salty sea air as we pass the ocean. Here the blue of the sky is merged with the blue of the sea. I want to run to it. I want to have a baptism and be cleansed of my sinful thoughts. The same thoughts that drowned out the claps from passengers that sounded through the aircraft as we touched the runway hours before, with headscarves, bonnets and sports caps in abundance. We pass a church, then another, and another seconds later. Faith Temple Assembly of God. Calvary Baptist Church. New Testament Church of God. We pass a makeshift shack with a weathered corrugated roof. Pineapples covered in plastic hang from the structure like earrings; its wooden shelves are filled with rows of ripe mangoes, papayas and guavas. The seller of the fruit is a woman with a baby boy in her lap. He sucks on her left breast. I turn away.

Irie FM sounds as we make our way from Montego Bay to Mandeville through the winding roads marked with deep potholes. Raymond's driving gives me motion sickness. I ask him for a sheet from the *Jamaica Gleaner* sprawled out on the back seat. One year, on a trip to Negril with my cousins from Canada, the car packed with jerk chicken, coco bread and sorrel in a cooler, Grandad told us that sitting on newspaper whilst in the car helped ease the discomfort. It always did, and I never thought to ask why.

'Yuh ah big woman now, Miss Sharna, very pretty,' says Raymond above the steady four-beat rhythm of the reggae sounds. 'You have husband yet?' I half smile and say no, without qualification, trying to change the subject. He is relentless and says, 'Don't wait too long now, Miss Sharna, as a woman, unnuh eggs dem dry up.'

I do not reply, and stare out of the window.

We drive further into the interior. I take in the shades of green that make up the landscape: lime, parakeet, with pockets of seaweed and sage. I recognise the wide leaves of the banana trees that garnish the hills like a scene from a postcard. At their centre is a hand of curved skins. I am reminded of childhoods spent on the one-acre plot of land behind Grandad's house which he bought for farming – a reconnection to his life before leaving Jamaica for England aged twenty. One year, after showing me where he had planted rows of carrots, pumpkins and Irish potatoes, he pointed to the green banana patch and told me it was 'good fi boil the banana ina the skin, because it very rich in iron'. It was during that same conversation that he taught me how to delicately separate the poisonous black seeds from the yellow ackee that looked to me like scrambled eggs. I watched him with a laser focus as I sucked on the soft coral flesh of guineps and peeled sweet oranges in the hot sun. He is the reason I bought a house with a garden to plant fruit and vegetables when I was twenty-four. I am filled with regret. 'Yuh never call, what a way yuh throw mi away' are the words that echo in my head. I lie and tell myself these two weeks will make up for the calls not made and the calls unreturned over the last few years of law school, all the late nights in the office and my determination to make partner by thirty-five.

Two hours later, despite the occasionally bumpy ride, I rub away the dribble that has trickled from my mouth. I am more tired than usual. We turn right into Rosebury Road: we have arrived. We drive down the long asphalt drive, lined on either side with potted tropical flowers, aloe and pear trees, black mint, moringa and starry thyme. Strangely, I miss the sound of the dogs barking. There isn't the usual rush of adrenaline, the impending fear of coming face to face with Bruno, the largest of the dogs Grandad once had, who would run up to the vehicle and chew on the car's mudguards. He towered over the others like a horse and had a bark that filled me with dread. The dogs were poisoned years ago in an attempted house robbery and were never replaced. I feel a sense of loss. I never thought I would miss what I'd once feared. This memory is abruptly interrupted as Raymond says, 'We reach, Miss Sharna.' I thank him, though I do not comment on his driving that far exceeded any speed limit back home, nor do I mention the moments I was scared for my life, afraid of the car veering off the meandering mountain roads.

I take a few steps forward, walking over the terracotta drains in which both my younger cousin and I managed to get a leg stuck on separate occasions. It was during this same trip that Grandad decided he would retire permanently in Jamaica. The large bungalow is before me. It is no longer painted a cotton white but a light lavender, which I find unsettling. It looks incongruous with the Tuscan red thatched roof that is still intact.

Grandad. He is sat on the shiny, white-tiled veranda, framed by three arches. I notice the rocking chair is no longer there. 'Sharn, it's good to see you.' He smiles, his dentures shining through. 'Thank the Lawd for his journey mercies.' He does not comment on my locs or the tattoo I haven't bothered to hide. His hair is grey. A striking difference to the dyed jet black I am used to seeing. But it suits him. Aged eighty-nine, he still has a better hairline than most. His face looks the same, just shrunken in parts, sagging at the mouth. By his side is a walking stick I haven't seen before. He looks sunken in the chair, bent at the waist like an envelope. There is still a kindness to his smile which feels like home. I bend down, kiss him on the cheek and say, 'It's good to see you, Grandad, you look well.' He smiles, looking into my eyes. I haven't mentioned it, but I feel that he knows.

In the morning, I awake to the smell of fried breadfruit, ackee and saltfish, and plantain. I roll over. I'm overcome with nausea. It's now a familiar feeling. I put on the electric fan and brush away the beads of sweat on my forehead. I glance over to the dressing table lined with yellowed family photos and old Father's Day cards. I am met with a picture of myself six years ago, sitting in a chair, holding a cream scroll with a red ribbon attached to it. On my head is a black square hat. I am in a white dress and have a light blue sash across my torso to signify that I am a graduate of the University of Warwick. To my right is my aunt, and next to her stands my mother, who smiles with her whole mouth. It was her day really. The grand finale of years of sacrifice and debt on her part as she played the role of both parents, without the guidance of her own mother to show her how to do it. It was anticipation for this that kept her going during the cold nights when she would stare at the unoccupied space next to her in the bed. On my left is my best friend, Niah, and my lover, who is no longer my lover. It is a scene now that only exists in my memory and in this frame. I hold my belly, and then I sigh.

Aunty V, Grandad's second wife and not my mother's mother, calls me for breakfast. Grandad blesses the food but doesn't eat. 'Bless this food to our bodies for Christ sake, amen,' he says, closing in prayer. Before he left for England when I was four, in the days when he lived a ten-minute walk from my mum and me before we moved to Greenwich, he would read me one of my favourite stories before bed, either *So Much* or *A is for Ackee: A Jamaican A–Z*. After we had read the last page, ending with *Because they loved him SO MUCH* or *Z for Zest*, he would bend down with his once-strong knees, and together we would say the Lord's Prayer – the King James Version. It is still something I do, but I haven't said grace in years. Aunty V doesn't eat either but busies herself in the kitchen. She moves slowly because of the heat, sweat dripping along the contours of her face. Though younger than Grandad, she has aged too. Her face is peppered with moles and there are patches of grey in her two braided cornrows. She is dressed for her trip to the market in a long denim skirt and a loose red blouse. I wonder how she will survive when he is gone. She has spent the last forty years being a wife to Grandad, with few interests of her own. 'Mi can't eat if him nuh eat. Him pain ah fi mi own,' she tells me. I feel sorry for her, then I envy her.

After breakfast, I unpack my suitcase. I place into the pantry cupboard the six tins of Heinz vegetable soup and

Reserve Port that Grandad requested I bring from 'h'gland'.
I join him on the veranda, having changed into a long green
dashiki, and settle in a plastic-covered wooden chair. I miss
the rocking chair. I channel my inner Caribbean elder and
sit in silence with him, watching as cars and people go by. A
herd of goats enter the drive and feast on pears that have
fallen from the tree. The front garden is full of the large
brown fruit. It seems excessive. I think of the artisan cafes
in Blackheath and the extortionate prices they charge for
avocado smashed on organic rye bread. If I wanted to, I
could have a pear for each hour of the day for the duration
of my trip, and there would still be plenty left. I think of
excess, waste and capitalism. I think of school fees on a
single salary. My head hurts. A lime-green butterfly flutters
by. Grandad inhales and says, 'Hallelujah, praise the Lawd,'
before getting up to read his Bible again for the day and to
pray.

Grandad tells me to join him in the spare room and asks
when I last went to church. I lie. Lying is easier than
explaining the inconsistencies I am forever grappling with.
Like how we spent over a year praying for my pastor's heal-
ing, with endless famous preachers declaring that they
would see him dance again. But he died anyway. So many
of us left church after that. 'You must go to church when it
opens up. These are the last and evil days,' he says. He
opens his leather-bound Bible, held together by thick
masking tape, worn after years of carrying it to endless

prayer and fasting meetings and the various Bible studies he led. He turns to his favourite passage, Psalm 27, and reads it aloud. '*The Lord is my light and my salvation; whom shall I fear? The Lord is the strength of my life; of whom shall I be afraid?* I am afraid of a lot. I am afraid of the future. Of Grandad's impending death. Of being a mother.

I haven't yet told him that I too have a ball of cells within me. They are not cancerous, but at eleven weeks the zygote has divided many times over and has implanted itself in the walls of my uterus. This is a baby I am not sure I want but do not have the courage to get rid of. This is not how things were supposed to be. Weeks before, when two lines appeared on the stick I had peed onto, I cried out in disappointment and fear. I am not ready to be a mother. I never wanted to be a single mother like my own.

Grandad prays and then takes a nap. I take one too.

I wake up to a mosquito biting my arm. It's nice to be wanted. To be devoured. To be needed for survival. To have someone want you, really want you. Need you so much it hurts. I watch as the insect continues to puncture my skin, feasting on my blood. I always imagined I would have a marriage like Grandad told me he and my late grandma had. I grew up sitting on Grandad's lap, when his legs were strong, listening to him tell stories of how, at a church meeting, he had prayed that God would send him a companion after seven single years in England working first in Sheffield as a cleaner, then in Birmingham as a bus driver and later in London at a car factory as a stocktaker. That night, he had a dream of meeting a woman from Barbados sat on a bench in Garratt Park. 'The very next day how mi see her in the dream is how mi see her ina real life,' is what he always told me, smiling, with tears in his eyes. I know he's been wanting to die since she was taken so violently by a stroke aged thirty-six. I wish I'd had the chance to meet her. It was a Hollywood-style romance. A pan-Caribbean love story bridging Barbados and Jamaica. A love I yearned for, but all I had was a back and forth with a man who loved me less than I loved him. It is the reason my mum and I no longer speak. She was right and I was wrong. She could see the signs from the first time we met at university. His comments and inconsistent behaviour, like the man that left her. I will forever be shackled to him because of the night after my friend Jada's barbecue. The evening where I had too many glasses of wine, followed by a drunken conversation that would change everything.

We have dinner at 3 p.m. Aunty V has made rice and peas, brown stew chicken, yam, sweet potato and callaloo. I have been vegan for a number of years now, but I reason that the chicken here is not pumped with hormones. I do not blame it on my raging cravings. Aunty V brings Grandad a plate of two boiled plantains and a piece of yam, no meat in sight. It reminds me of baby food. I watch him eat. I want to offer to help and steady his shaking hand, but I can't find the right words. Instead, I think of his last visit when I was still at university. I came back to London one weekend and we cooked together at my mum's house. He made his peppered rump steak special, I made the hard food – boiled dumpling, yam and green banana to have with steamed cabbage. Together we baked my favourite, coconut cake with extra vanilla essence. I wonder when he last prepared a meal for himself. He eats half a plantain and then says, 'Mi belly can't tek the other one and a half, it weak.' He takes a sip of tea from his favourite green mug with a chip on its side and moves to the settee.

Later, we watch the news at 6 p.m. For as long as I can remember, Grandad has always watched the evening news without fail. I find the Jamaican ads jarring. There is too much excitement for advertising Wi-Fi and life insurance. There is a reminder from the 'Ministry of Health and Wellness' on the importance of eating well and exercise, and to 'love yuh body, treat yuh body right'. One, two, three; bronze, silver and gold at the Olympics. I feel a sense of pride, though I am just a quarter Jamaican and refer to myself as Black British. I know very little about my Ugandan side. My dad disappeared before I learnt how to say those three-letter words, which to me have no meaning. After the news headlines again at 8 p.m., Grandad changes the channel to God TV. I get up to cut a slice of rum and raisin cake to have with non-dairy ice cream, avoiding the sermon. I overhear an American preacher quote from Revelations 13. There is mention of vaccinations and the mark of the beast. I roll my eyes. 'The preacher man foolish,' Grandad mutters under his breath. I am surprised, then I laugh.

The next morning there is a knock on my door. 'Mi need yuh to drive me to the lawyers,' says Grandad. 'Mi can't drive, the foot dem weak.' The appointment is at ten, but we leave at nine even though the journey is only ten minutes away. I am reminded that my punctuality comes from Grandad. He enters the beige Jeep slowly, with a pronounced arch in his back, resting heavily on his walking stick that I am still not used to seeing. I remember that the reason I am here in Jamaica, after all these years, is because his days are numbered. I cast my mind to fonder memories.

'Grandad,' I say, 'do you remember when you let me sit on your lap in the car and drive up and down the drive when I was younger?'

He settles in his seat and takes off his khaki cap before putting on his seat belt and says, 'Yes, Sharn, I remember.' He laughs with his whole mouth, which reminds me of my mother.

We have barely been in the car for five minutes, yet Grandad is overly cautious and critical of my driving: 'Look both ways, Sharn', 'Don't go too too fass, man.' I try to hide my annoyance, having had my licence for more than five years. But Grandad telling me to look both ways triggers a memory. '*Look both ways before crossing over.*' It is a line from the song he would sing on the days he picked me up from school when my mum worked lates. My hand in his, we would cross the road and walk to the corner shop opposite my primary school, where he would buy me a mix of cola bottles and fizzy strawberry laces and a packet of Tunes for him, though he didn't have a sore throat. He says it again: 'Look both ways, Sharn, not too fass.' And this time I smile.

When we arrive, we wait. Waiting. Always waiting. There is no sense of urgency. In Jamaica, I am forced to be still.

THIS IS THE LAST WILL AND TESTAMENT of me, REGINALD THOMAS of Rosebury Road, Mandeville Post Office in the parish of Manchester, retired stocktaker. Grandad has put me down as the joint executor of his will with my mother. My law degree from a top university and career as a corporate lawyer makes me the sensible one in the family, though I am far from that. I read through the document looking for errors and any inconsistencies, resurrecting the knowledge gained from a two-week university module in wills, trusts and estates. I ask for it to be sent to me via email to conduct a final check.

Back at home, whilst Grandad is sleeping, I spend another early afternoon on the veranda, this time with a soy patty in hand. The last time I came to Jamaica, it was the second year of my plant-based eating. My decision had been fuelled principally by vanity as opposed to animal welfare – my girl Gabby had said going vegan was the reason she no longer had acne. 'I don't eat meat any more, Grandad,' I said on my first night sat on the veranda, the trills of crickets in the background. 'What? Not even mutton?' he asked, leaning forward in the rocking chair. I laughed so hard. 'No, Grandad, not even mutton.' The day after his trip to the bank, he returned from Juici with a soy patty in place of my usual beef. I wish I'd told him then how much I loved him. Earlier this morning, though, it was Aunty V who asked me if I wanted a chicken or beef patty. Just as she got into her taxi to go to the supermarket, I reminded her that my preference was the meat-free option. I was overcome with sorrow. Grandad buying me soy patties with a bottle of Ting is something I will never experience again.

A multitude of ants appears from out of nowhere and devour the yellow crumbs that have fallen onto the tiles. The bright sun shines for the first time in days and the red bites on my arm glisten in the daylight. I take back what I said about liking the mosquitoes. They're a bitch. It's astounding how something so small can cause you so much pain. '*Likkle but tallawah*', as the Jamaican proverb goes. I then think of the cyst on Grandad's abdomen and the fertilised embryo within me. I resist the urge to scratch and stand up. I walk to the front garden in search of a rosette of triangular aloe leaves, which I find by the orange tree that no longer bears fruit. I find a broad leaf, fleshy, thick and with spiky, serrated edges. I cut off a piece and slice it open with a kitchen knife. Inside is a slimy gel, which I rub along the red bumps on my arms and legs, like my mum did for me when I was a child. I feel instant relief. I then take it to my mouth and it tastes the worst type of bitter, a mix of spinach and acid. Back when Grandad's legs were strong he would return from his morning walks at 6 a.m. and blend aloe vera with Guinness, fresh oranges and raw eggs, and drink it every morning. He was such a health-conscious man, but it didn't stop the cancer. I think about how much I hate the pharmaceutical industry for failing my grandfather. I try not to think about how much I hate God for letting him down.

Later that night, I toss and turn. I remember the call from the oncologist a few hours before. She confirmed with a more extensive diagnosis that because of Grandad's age, there is no point in doing chemotherapy. That the treatment will be too aggressive. She said to make the most of the time we have now. That he has anywhere between six months and two years. Perhaps less. Her words make me think of death and then life. In that order. She recommended that he takes guinea hen weed as a tea. I reach for my phone and google it. It can be used to fight cancerous cells. Further down on the page I read that it can be used to induce abortions. My mind wanders again to the list of pros and cons I drafted to try and reach a decision. I ended up with two columns of equal weighting.

I should call. No, maybe a text is better: *Hey David, I hope you're well. I'm not quite sure how to say this. I'm pregnant and it's yours. I haven't decided what to do yet.* I think to text Niah; she has always been good with words. But I feel bad. It's been difficult balancing work and spending time with my best friend. There was a time we saw one another every day, at school and at university, but I know I haven't been there when she's needed me most. I leave the message to David in my drafts. I don't send it. I tell myself he has moved on. I have seen from socials that he is living his best life in Accra and Dubai. I am frustrated with my flesh again. A moment filled with want has led me here. A cockroach scurries along the wall. A younger me would have cried out in terror. I realise there are scarier things in life.

At five, I wake up in a pool of sweat and tears. I dreamt that the baby inside me was snatched from my womb. There was a flash of bright light that hovered above me; it had a human face. It was the face of Grandad but a younger version. I am afraid but then I am overcome by a grave sense of overprotectiveness. Of protecting what is mine.

Thirsty, I head to the kitchen to get some water from the fridge. Grandad lies in the room he uses for prayer. He is already up and dressed for the day in slightly worn suit trousers and a short-sleeved white shirt. I realise I have never seen him in pyjamas. On the days he would make me a bowl of cornmeal porridge with nutmeg and cinnamon before school, he was always dressed so formally. His Bible is on his lap. I walk into the room and take a seat at the end of the bed, and I ask him how he slept. 'Mi not too wonderful, Sharn, mi feeling weak, weak. Weak in the tummy, and the foot dem weak.'

I don't know what to say. What do you say to a man who is at death's door? I notice an imprint of a dead mosquito, its blood smeared on the wall.

'What is man?' Grandad says. I realise it's a rhetorical question. 'Man is like trash.' I think I've heard him incorrectly. He stops briefly before continuing. '*As for man, his days are like grass. As a flower of the field, so he flourishes.*'

I recognise the scripture. The words are written on my heart and bound around my neck, despite my best intentions to forget them. They are learnt from many years in Sunday school. I wish they had explained to us how to wrestle with doubts about our faith in our twenties. But they didn't. A soft breeze passes through the house.

'The cancer, it took mi uncle. I was sitting on one seat like how you sit and him looking up and say, "They coming at twelve o'clock. Yes, Reg, them coming at twelve o'clock." And then at twelve him die.'

'They?' I ask.

'Yes,' he says, 'The angels dem.' I think of how cancer runs in the family and how it will take me out. 'Yes, Farda, praise the Lawd,' he says after a few moments. 'Mi nuh have long, Sharn,' he says.

I am silent. He is silent too. He has always been a man of

few words. I move to lay next to him and without words I say, *I'm sorry. I'm sorry I didn't come before.*

It's as though he hears me because he says, 'It's awrite, Sharn.' He opens his worn Bible. He tells me he is going to have a little time of encouragement and prayer. He sits up and turns to 1 Peter 4:8. He reads the passage aloud: '*Above all, love each other deeply, because love covers over a multitude of sins.*' I don't know why, but I start crying.

'Grandad, I'm pregnant.' It comes out before I realise what I have said.

'I know, Sharn. Mi see it ina dream.' He puts his arm around me. 'It awrite, Sharna. It awrite.'

This is not the reaction I anticipated. I expected a response cloaked in holiness-tradition dogma, that I would be berated for having a child outside of marriage. My salt tears wet his shirt. I cry because I realise he would have supported me during the pregnancy but most likely won't be here to see me through. I cry for the life I don't feel equipped to raise. I cry because I want my mother.

'A child is a gift. A gift from the Lawd. And yuh 'ave yuh mudda. A child needs their mudda. And their faada.' I think of David. 'Make peace with your mudda,' he continues. 'I have been praying, always praying for you and she. It's OK, Sharn. Trust in the Lawd.'

As I wipe my tears, Grandad starts to sing softly. '*When peace like a river attendeth my way.*' They are the verses from his favourite hymn, which I have heard him sing many times before. No piano sounds, but there is a depth to his baritone that fills the room. I think first of my mother. And then of this supposed gift. Of the potential of a reality beyond termination. I think of the possibility that the baby within me is a he. I think of him bearing Grandad's name. Reggie.

BLOOD AND INK

To call it love at first sight would be tiresome, lazy even. So perhaps it was love at first sound. Love at the cadence of her voice and the symphony of her breath, when Tariq first heard Ifey read her words aloud. It was a softness, like a lullaby, with perfect enunciation and pauses in the right places. But also like the crescendo of waves on a shore. He thought her voice sounded like water. He wanted to speak to her. He wanted to find out about her sources of inspiration. And whether it was the case that, like him, she felt most herself in words. But before he had the chance, she disappeared. Just her name printed in black felt-tip, folded on a sheet of paper. Tariq found comfort, however, in knowing he would be able to speak to her the following week. He would remind her of his name, and maybe make a joke, to see the joy in her eyes again. But he didn't see her the following week. He wouldn't see her again for months.

The day Tariq had fallen in love with Ifey's voice, she hadn't even noticed him. Instead, she had been trying to suppress her rising unease. It was the first time in over a year that she was in a room full of strangers. She hated attending events, gatherings and after-work drinks, which were always a trigger for her anxiety. She had welcomed the lockdowns, which had enabled her to avoid situations that made her feel awkward, or worse, humiliated. And she'd finally had the time and space to return to the thing she loved most: putting pen to paper and pouring out the novel that had previously existed only in her mind. She'd even responded to the call to tweet a 280-character pitch, which had led to an agent sliding into her DMs and requesting a sample of the manuscript. So when her friend Niah sent her a link to a programme of writing workshops, suggesting they go along together, she signed up, not realising they'd be in person as opposed to online. This was how she found herself sitting in a classroom full of people she did not know, fear bubbling inside her.

But as the session went on, and after her friend finally arrived from work, Ifey began to feel lighter, with words falling effortlessly from her mind onto the page. And because she almost felt like herself, her best self, she offered to read out her work. It was not something she would normally do, but in this environment she felt different – comfortable – and, for once, in control. So she read, bringing her words to life. Her peers praised her reading, which gave her a feeling of something akin to contentment, a sort of inner strength. She remembered that she knew herself best in words.

But as quickly as those feelings came, they were replaced by a familiar abhorrent sensation. There was a crushing in her abdomen and what felt like the dragging down of her insides. Of unrelenting sharp knives being thrust into her uterus, spreading to her lower back and thighs. She knew what would follow. She could not risk the embarrassment that had marked so many of her teenage years. And so, after her tutor had given instructions for the final exercise, she stood up, gathered her belongings and left. Finding the toilet, she ran inside a cubicle without time to lock the door. She vomited. Her bowels loosened. And then came the flow of blood between her legs. Minutes later, she blacked out.

Ifey woke up to an unsettling blend of sterile white light and the smell of antiseptic. Disorientated, she realised she was lying on a rigid mattress, with various red and blue tubes inserted into her left arm. She panicked. But then came the gentle chatter of voices she recognised.

'Guys?' Ifey groaned, her eyes slightly vacant.

'Ifey, you're awake, thank God,' said Niah, standing up and walking over to the bed.

'Where am I?' she asked.

'You're in hospital, babe,' said Sharna, the third girl in Ifey's secondary school friendship group.

'What?' murmured Ifey. 'What happened?'

'You fainted and hit your head. You've been out for hours,' said Niah.

'Hours?' repeated Ifey, confused.

'Yeah, you had a concussion,' said Sharna.

Ifey noticed a dull ache in her temples and a throbbing lump on her forehead. As her senses returned, she became aware of the fire within. 'I don't understand, how did you know?'

'After you left the class, I came to look for you,' said Niah. As Ifey's oldest friends, she and Sharna knew what her periods could do to her.

'God, how embarrassing,' said Ifey, the events of the evening starting to come back.

'I'm so sorry, but it could have been so much worse,' said Niah. 'Thank God you're OK.'

Some time later, after Sharna had left for Ifey's flat to pick up a change of clothes and toiletries and the nurses had run various tests, a doctor entered the room. She looked a similar age to Ifey, who noticed her fresh ombre braids and lilac Crocs at once. 'Hi, Ifey, I'm Dr Akwetey. How are you feeling?' she asked, taking a seat in the chair Sharna had vacated.

Ifey spoke of her head pain and the intense abdominal cramps. She mentioned that just before she fainted she had been overcome with nausea and had the sudden urge to vomit and pass watery stools, permanent features of her periods for as long as she could remember. She explained that she'd always had severe backache, with her legs going numb, and as a teenager had been given mefenamic acid, which had done nothing to help. She talked about how she'd noticed a change recently. That on the other side of twenty-five, there seemed to be an even greater punishment for failing to fertilise an egg each month: blood in her faeces, bloating, constipation, extreme exhaustion, and pain so debilitating she thought she would die.

After the doctor had listened to Ifey, offering sympathetic smiles and nods, she made a few notes on her clipboard. Then she revealed the diagnosis that Ifey wished she had received years ago: endometriosis.

The week after Ifey finally had the language to describe her pain, Tariq was back in the creative writing class. Ever since he'd heard Ifey read out her work, he had been hoping he would see her again. He wanted to talk about her writing. He wanted to ask why she'd chosen to use the second-person perspective and not the first or third. Whether it was because she had found it more immersive, akin to spoken word or poetry, or if she had been inspired by a writer who had used the same technique. But the next session came and went and she was not there. He figured that maybe she had been on holiday or had an engagement at work. When she did not turn up for the third week, however, he thought that maybe she was unwell. He found himself concerned for her welfare even though he didn't know her. But when their class entered its second month and she still hadn't come back, he concluded that she wasn't going to return. He told himself that this was good. That she had most likely secured a book deal so no longer needed the sessions. He figured that she was on her way to realising the dream they all shared: to become a published author. He was grateful he'd had a chance to bask in her art and could one day say he'd had the pleasure of hearing her read her work at the back of a classroom in the West End.

In the weeks that followed, he focused on why he had signed up for the class in the first place. He reminded himself that he was saying yes to his art, and making space in his life for the thing that brought him joy. He was honing his craft, becoming the best writer he could be. He was reading even more widely: short stories, poetry, and narrative non-fiction. And for the first time in his life, he was surrounded by people who were also lovers of words, appreciating the art form. It was refreshing. But though he was grateful for this new element of joy in his life, he wondered from time to time about the woman whose voice sounded like water. What she was up to, what she was doing, what she was writing.

Ifey was in bed when she opened the letter detailing her scheduled surgery. Though she was relieved she now knew what was wrong with her, she found herself drowning in memories. Like the time she had vomited on the train on her way into work and, mortified, had got off at the next stop, deciding to walk to work, arriving an hour late for her meeting. Or the time at university when she was sprawled out on the shower floor, crippled with pain, missing one of her final-year exams. Then there was the time she'd thrown up and passed out moments after being seated at Sharna's sixteenth birthday meal at Chiquito in Leicester Square.

She felt angry. She thought of all the times she had been told she was being dramatic. Of the ways her concerns had always been dismissed, leaving her perpetually frustrated. She thought of the times when she was in so much agony she had more than once contemplated taking her own life.

Opening her laptop, she googled 'endometriosis'. The doctor had told her that this was almost certainly her diagnosis, but that she wanted to confirm with a laparoscopy. There were words and phrases that stood out to her: *No cure. Infertility.* She scrolled further down the screen. *Painful intercourse.* She thought about her ex. Sex with him had been painful, something to endure more than to enjoy. He had been her first, so she figured it was normal. She had no idea it was a result of tissue growing outside of her uterus, extending to her ovaries and fallopian tubes.

The anger built as Ifey thought of her GP, who hadn't taken the time to diagnose the problem when she made an appointment as a teenager but had suggested quickly that she went on the pill. She was angry that she had not advocated for herself, or asked for a second opinion, when she had been diagnosed with irritable bowel syndrome and then constipation in her mid twenties.

Ifey then thought about her writing. She wondered if the rising dread she'd felt before the class was actually down to her social anxiety. Maybe it had instead been something like an aura, a sign from within of what awaited her. A warning of what would follow. She wished she had listened. She was sure her classmates would have seen her being taken away in the ambulance. She imagined the worst, herself on a stretcher with blood and diarrhoea smeared down her legs. Though she remembered the joy she had experienced in feeling her confidence grow, she couldn't face going back. She rolled over and cried.

But as the weeks went on, Ifey tried to put what had happened behind her. She mulled over her diagnosis. She'd been through the various stages of grief, moving from denial and anger to acceptance. She thought about what the doctor had said. Now, with this diagnosis, she would be able to better manage her symptoms. She would be able to get the proper treatment. She was starting to feel encouraged by the accounts her friends sent her to follow on Instagram and TikTok of Black women and how they managed their condition. She drew on the strength of her teenage years and resolved not to let her body defeat her. She was determined to make this novel the best it could be. It wasn't that the pain had gone away. It hadn't. The difference now was that she knew what it was, and in some ways that felt empowering.

Niah had also reassured her that no one had seen her being taken away by the paramedics. Though she was anxious, she decided to return to the class. She emailed her tutor and explained that she had been sick but would love to come back if that was a possibility. Then Ifey returned to her notebook. She put pen to paper and worked on something new. She called it 'Blood and Ink'.

When Tariq saw Ifey walk through the classroom door, he was overcome with surprise and then delight. He had been certain he would never see her again. She looked slightly nervous, her shoulders tense, her eyes downcast. She was holding a purple leather-bound notebook that looked handmade. She was even more beautiful than he remembered. He had been so taken by her voice that he hadn't noticed the dark mahogany of her eyes or the distinct smell of her perfume. He watched as she took a seat next to the woman who had invited him to a new collective for Black writers. He realised now that the two women shared a connection outside of this space. Like they did life together. He found that he was envious of Niah, in having such a connection. But he was grateful to see Ifey again.

'Welcome back, everyone,' said the creative writing tutor as they settled in their chairs. 'I hope you all had a good week off. And welcome back to Ifey. It's great to have you again.'

The session began as usual with a free-writing exercise, everyone reading out their work at the end. Tariq listened intently to Ifey, in awe again of the musicality of her voice. As she neared the end of her monologue, he decided that she was his favourite author. When it was his turn to give feedback, he was lost for words. And so he settled on 'That was beautiful,' though it was a mere mumble under his breath. He watched her reaction to his words. She looked freer, more at ease.

When the class came to an end, he knew he needed to speak to her. Though he was never really one to have to game like some of his friends, he had a way with people. His personality always shone through. And so he walked over to Ifey as she was picking up her bag. 'Good to see you again,' he said, and realised he should have started with something else, something more meaningful. He continued. 'I loved what you shared today. It was really powerful.'

'Thanks so much,' said Ifey.

'Is it part of a novel you're working on?'

'Yeah, it is actually.'

'I would love to read some more of it. If that's cool with you.'

'Really?' she said, shocked.

'Really,' he said with a smile.

Ifey hesitated but said, 'OK, what's your email?'

As Ifey reached into her bag to get her phone, Tariq noticed that Niah was smiling too.

It began as a conversation, from one writer to another. Ifey had shared the first few chapters of her new novel with Tariq and he had got back to her in just a few hours. She wasn't used to someone taking an interest in her art. She was not used to someone taking an interest in her full stop. But it was nice to meet someone who, like her, understood that writing was sacred. Someone who understood that writing was a spiritual experience, with the ability to transform and heal. He seemed to see the world like she did and understood that writing was the gift that kept on giving. He always wanted to know what she was working on next, and gave the most affirming feedback. He seemed to like her mind. And she liked his too. She loved how he experimented with both form and genre, and subverted literary conventions. She was taken by his discipline and dedication to the craft. She loved how he made her want to be a better writer. She loved how he was beginning to brighten her world, sparking even more creativity in her, like sunlight. Weeks went by before they moved from email to an exchange of numbers, and she realised that maybe it wasn't only his mind she was interested in. She found herself looking forward to their discussions in the realms of blue and grey, and put extra effort into her appearance for their classes. But still she worried that going any further would risk ruining the connection they already shared.

And Tariq felt the same way too. Speaking with Ifey felt like peace. Something about her made him think of the ocean: her serenity, her depth, her mystery. For years now, he had longed for a deeper, more meaningful connection with a romantic partner, but his previous relationships had left him disappointed and unfulfilled. Talking to Ifey was different: it felt like he was talking to himself. He thought this was perhaps what it was like to have a kindred spirit, finding home in someone. But he didn't say any of this to her. Like Ifey, he didn't want to ruin what they had.

But he was curious. He wanted to know her. And he wanted to know why she had missed so many sessions of their writing classes. So one evening, he took a deep breath and asked.

*

Ifey looked at the message from Tariq for some time. She was reluctant to share this part of herself with him. She thought about keeping it light. She could lie and say she'd had a bad flu of sorts, but that would not explain why she had been away for close to two months. She wasn't sure how he would take the truth. Her ex-boyfriend had always been uncomfortable when she spoke about her periods. He had also been quick to belittle her pain. But things were different now: she had the language for what was wrong. She felt stronger and more in control. Ifey started typing. Then she stopped. She decided to call him instead.

'Wow, Ifey. That sounds awful. I'm so sorry,' said Tariq after she had shared the most vulnerable part of herself. As he continued to speak, she was met with tenderness so soft, she thought she might cry. For the first time, someone had really listened to her. And though Tariq would never know her pain, he had made the effort to understand. It was more than empathy: she felt seen. Once the call ended, she suddenly wanted to spend more time with the man who was capturing her mind. She picked up her phone and messaged him: *Would you be down to meet up outside our class? Just us two?*

After their coffee together at a bookshop, Ifey and Tariq walked for hours in a park, side by side, their fingers occasionally touching, their hands not quite interlocking. They discussed the intricacies of their writing as a craft. The importance of conflict and suspense, the multiplicities of form and the benefits of different points of view. But he wanted to know more about her; she wanted to know what he liked and what he loved. They were yearning to know more about each other.

On this perfect day, as the sun shone brightly, they sat on the grass, their legs brushing each other's, their words punctured only by the sound of parakeets and the shouts of a group of friends playing football nearby. After Tariq had read Ifey a few pages of his favourite anthology, he paused and said, 'I got you something.'

'Seriously?' said Ifey, taken aback. She wasn't used to open displays of affection.

Tariq picked up his tote bag and took out a lilac leather-bound notebook. 'For you,' he said, handing it to her.

'Oh my goodness,' said Ifey. IFEY AKINYEMI was embossed in gold on the front of the notebook in her favourite colour. She opened the book to the front page. There was a hand-written note that said *To Ifey, you are a brilliant writer, keep writing. Love Tariq x*. Her eyes filled with water. 'Thank you so much, I love it,' she said and hugged him, trying not to cry.

They had been talking and laughing for what felt like forever when Tariq said, 'So, I wanted to ask you something.'

'Go on,' Ifey said, taking a sip of the pink lemonade he'd bought for her. Tariq took her hand in his. 'We've been talking for a while now.'

Ifey returned his smile. But then she felt something within. It was not a flutter of butterflies like before. Instead it was a deep, sharp pang stretching from her abdomen to her thighs and lower back that came violently and without warning.

Tariq continued. 'I really like you. Like, a lot.'

Ifey remembered how she had looked at her period app before she left the house. She wasn't due for another few days, but her periods were always unpredictable. Never on time, always late. They were never early.

There was a visible shift in Ifey's demeanour. 'You OK, Ifey?' asked Tariq.

Hours before, when she had closed the app, she had felt anxious but had ignored it, desperate to see Tariq. But she knew now that had been her body trying to warn her, just like before.

'I think I'm going to . . .' said Ifey, and stopped. She had ways of describing what was happening to her now. She started again. 'I'm having a flare-up.'

Tariq shifted on the grass and put a hand on her shoulder, his eyes heavy with concern.

'I'm really sorry,' said Ifey. Though she had told Tariq about her condition, she did not want him to see her like this. It was her burden to bear, and not his. 'I need to go,' she said, sitting up.

'It's OK. I'm here.' It was such tenderness in the midst of violence.

'Sometimes, I . . .' said Ifey, but she was unable to finish her sentence. She felt a discomfort in the right side of her abdomen, and the usual burning in her bladder. She took a deep breath. 'Sometimes, I . . .'

Next came the dizziness. Before her vision blurred, she managed, 'Call an ambulance.'

It was déjà vu. Ifey awoke to an unfamiliar setting, completely disorientated. She expected to find herself surrounded by her closest friends as before, but instead Tariq was by her bedside. 'Ifey,' he said softly. 'How are you feeling?'

But before she had a chance to respond, the doctor came in. 'Hey, Ifey, good to see you again. Well, not good, but you know what I mean,' said Dr Akwetey. She had on another pair of Crocs Ifey had not seen before. They were high-tops and had a zip. 'I am so sorry this has happened to you again. But the good news is that your surgery has now been pushed forward and you have been marked as a priority. You should receive an update in the next few weeks.'

'Will that be a laparoscopy?' asked Tariq.

'Yes, that's right, most likely an ablation,' said the doctor, looking impressed. 'I'll be back shortly to check your vitals.

You didn't have any head trauma this time, thanks to Mr Man here, which is amazing. Just get lots of rest,' said the doctor, before leaving the room.

Ifey again looked at Tariq. He pulled a chair closer to the bed. 'How did you know about all of that?' she said.

'I did a bit of research.' He smiled and said, 'OK, maybe I did a fair bit.'

'Really?'

'Really.'

Ifey felt heat rise to her cheeks. She changed the subject and said, 'Thanks so much for being here. So sorry you had to see all of that, I—'

Tariq stopped her. 'There's honestly nothing to apologise for. I've got you.'

Ifey wasn't sure what to say, so she smiled.

Tariq looked at her for some time and then said, 'Ifey, I really care about you.' His words were failing him. He started again. 'That first time I met you, I honestly thought you were the most amazing woman and I didn't even know you properly. I barely knew your name.'

He moved closer and took her hand in his. It was the biggest risk he would ever take. He kissed her on the forehead. Ifey breathed deeply, tears welling up. Then she looked up at him and their eyes met. She leaned towards him and planted a kiss on his lips.

*

Years later, weeks after the launch of Tariq's debut novel and a month before Ifey signed with a literary agent, they would stand together on a raised platform, framed by the sun and the sea. Tariq would begin, 'To my favourite author . . .', to which those seated would laugh and then smile. He would continue, 'To my favourite person, *my* person, to the one whose voice sounded like water. I am grateful to the universe for bringing us together.'

Ifey would turn to him and smile. She would take it all in. Her vows would speak of love in perfect alignment. The two of them balancing each other out, both sun and ocean. Brought together because they both knew themselves best in words.

A SHORT TRIP TO TESCO

It is a Wednesday late afternoon, and you're in Tesco Extra attempting to rectify Veganuary. The start of what should have been a month of plant-based eating has really been plant-based plus chicken, fish and at times cheese, though you are lactose-intolerant.

You are near the back of the self-checkout line that snakes around the corner for a few metres. In your trolley is a packet of meat-free meatballs, vegan cheese and wholegrain spaghetti – the items you entered the store for – plus a bar of Lindt dark chocolate with a dash of sea salt, mango and chilli chutney poppadoms, and various other items you do not need. You are a slave to the Tesco Clubcard, though you passionately deny it. You think it is in your interest: £2.50, if not more, deducted from your shopping bill. But the multinational retailer is just collecting data about you: your shopping habits, your spending, your vices. You push your trolley a little further forward, getting closer to the beginning of the line, when you see him.

It is a weird feeling. Happiness spreads through you. Almost like seeing an old friend whom you haven't seen in years, but not quite. The pandemic had done that, caused you to miss people who were once part of your everyday life. You didn't know the particularities of who they were, their hopes, their dreams, their struggles. You didn't know their favourite colour or where they lived. You didn't even know their name, yet you sometimes found yourself wondering if they had survived the last two years. You had no way of knowing. You didn't have their number and you didn't follow each other on socials. Sometimes you thought of them, but by the second year of rising and falling Covid cases, U-turns in lockdown rules and government parties, somehow you had forgotten. But now you're back, and you are happy to see them after so long.

His locs are longer than you remember. They look fresh, like they have just been retwisted with lime and mango locking gel. You spot his two silver teeth and think back to the time he called you 'Empress'. It made you cringe, and then it reminded you of your favourite Antiguan uncle on your mother's side, and then of Chronixx.

He is perched on a high chair, speaking to one of the many Black security guards who safeguard what is, in your

eyes, the heart of Woolwich (OG Woolwich, not the gentrified side). You want him to turn around and see you, so you
lower your face mask slightly. With both your glasses and
surgical mask on, he may not recognise you. Your hair isn't
your usual waist-length knotless braids, and you've cut
your natural hair short. 'New year, new me,' you'd said,
aware of the cliche. The last two years have been tough, but
you wanted the transformation on the inside to match the
one on the outside. In a whole panoramic you came out to
your parents, moved out of your childhood home, got a
new job, and found a new love. For the first time in forever,
you are happy.

You think his name is Khari, but you aren't sure. You
don't think you have ever told him yours. You're not certain
when you first started speaking to each other. Over the
years, and after frequent impromptu trips to Tesco before
getting on your bus home from work or random nights of
jumping in your car, craving anything high in saturated fat
or sugar, you discussed an array of topics. It started off with
surface-level conversation, and then you ventured into
deeper subjects: wanting more out of life, and the existence
of what he called 'the big man upstairs'. You once chal-
lenged him on his hypermasculine and misogynistic leanings when he said that he would be cool to let a man cut his
hair at the barbers, but he wouldn't let a man retwist his
locs. 'But how does that make sense?' you asked him as you
scanned through a bag of onion rings, sweet and salt

popcorn and a bottle of rosé. 'It's too intimate. Just like I wouldn't let a man give me a massage, bruv.' He's problematic, problematic as hell. But there is a tenderness to him. You didn't realise it before, but these are the moments you have missed.

The security guard walks away. Finally, he turns around. 'Yoo, wagwan, sis,' he says, his two silver teeth shining through.

'Khari, good to see you. I thought you'd left.'

'Nah, still here, not as much though,' he says. He doesn't correct you, and you are proud of yourself for not forgetting his name. 'I normally do morning shifts. It's been a minute.'

You fall into an easy rhythm, like no time has passed at all. Like it hasn't been nearly two years since you have seen each other. There is laughter, and you see the kindness in his eyes that you have missed. 'Your hair,' you say. 'It looks so good. What did you do?'

'Vitamin E and A and them man, and scalp massages,' he says.

'I love that,' you smile.

You want to find out more. You want to start the locs journey at some point yourself, but he says, 'You good though, yeah?'

You don't give a full exposé of the last few years. Only of where you are now. Of the good times. 'I'm well,' you say. 'Just living my life really.'

'Living your best life, yeah? You still travelling and that?'

'Yup, Mexico in a few weeks actually.'

'Yoo, that's lit. You fully vaxxed?'

'Yeah, I've got both jabs, not the booster though. What about you?'

'I don't believe in them tings. Never had, not even when I was younger.'

You've heard this before. From members of your extended family who send pictures and videos full of misinformation to the various WhatsApp group chats. And their claims of never taking any vaccines in their life, forgetting about their jabs for tetanus and polio, or the first, second and third doses for protection against measles, mumps and rubella when they were children.

'But you had the BCG in school though, right?'

'Nah, not even. My dad's a Rasta and was always on the herbal flex. My kids haven't had them either.'

'Ah yeah, you've got three kids, right?'

'Nah, nah. Three kids is a lot. Two.'

'Two, three, same difference,' you say, and immediately you regret it. You think of your sister's experience of becoming a parent of two and then three – there is a big difference.

'Nah, it's not the same. Anyway, you're younger than me, init.'

You struggle to see the relevance, whether he is talking about the jabs or the lack of children that you do not want;

you are happy being an aunty to five. 'How old are you?' you ask, with a tinge of accusation.

'Twenty-eight,' he replies.

'I'm twenty-eight next week.'

'Happy birthday for next week. I'm still older than you though.'

You cannot believe he is pushing this point at his big age, and you laugh sarcastically.

He leaves momentarily. He verifies that the customer who has a bottle of Prosecco in their basket looks over twenty-five.

You move forward in the line and make your way to the only available self-checkout counter. As you are scanning your packet of meatless meatballs he returns. 'You are getting old though,' he says.

'No way. I'm still young. Just tryna make my dreams come true.'

'Yeah? Doing what?'

'Travelling, scriptwriting. I got onto a programme for new scriptwriters last week.'

'Sick! What's your script about?'

'Black love and friendship during the pandemic.'

'That's wavey. Did you find love in lockdown?'

'I did actually.' You met Destiny at a barbecue last summer, not long after you'd told your parents you'd never liked boys. And you knew straight away that she was your person. 'But I got the inspo before that. I know a lot of people who have met their partners on Hinge.'

'Hinge, yeah? The mandem keep telling me to jump on that.'

'You should. It's worked for a lot of people.'

'I hear it, but I just don't want my face on the internet like that.'

Hinge is hardly the internet, you think, as you scan the bar of dark chocolate and place it in the bagging area.

He continues, 'It is mad though. It's been so long since I've moved to a girl. Like when I see a girl on road, I don't know what to do any more. I just smile and keep it moving.' A customer calls for his assistance. They need help selecting the original glazed doughnut that they cannot find on the system. He comes back after a few moments and says, 'Like, I went to a club last week with my guys and I don't know what to do any more. And plus, these young girls look mad older now, you get me? The wig ting, the make-up, it's a lot.'

'I feel you. I'm always getting mistaken for a seventeen-year-old. Especially when I'm in a tracksuit, with no make-up on. It's long,' you say, scanning your packet of poppadoms.

He laughs. 'Nah, it's a good thing, still. Black don't crack and that.'

You agree. 'I've learnt to accept it, to be honest. But for real though, you should jump on Hinge.'

'You think?'

'Yeah, you should.' You feel back to your normal self. You want to do something nice, release some good vibes into the universe, so you say, 'I can help if you like. I can help with making a profile on Hinge if you want?'

'Yeah?'

'I'd be happy to. When do you normally take lunch?'

'Around one, for like an hour when I'm on the morning shift.'

Unlike a number of your friends' places of work, your office hasn't forced a new hybrid working policy. Your CEO said the company would continue to work from home as a standard, with monthly in-person team socials in the office, making substantial savings on building rent, which works absolutely fine for you.

'That's cool. I work a few days a week in Woolwich Works, so we can meet at Coffee Lounge by the square?'

'Sounds like a plan. I'm not working tomorrow, so Friday?'

'Friday at one ?' you say. 'Coffee and cake on me too.'

'Yeah calm. You a baller like that?'

'Nah, just feeling in a good mood,' you say.

'Them ones. What's your name again, sis?'

'Niecey,' you smile.

'Like short for Vaniece?'

'Yeah, but no one ever calls me that apart from my grand-mother, so don't.'

'Got you,' he laughs.

You scan your Clubcard, tap your Monzo to pay, and pack away your shopping.

'You gonna help me find love again, yeah?' he says, after walking back from removing the security tag from a customer's candle.

'I'll see what I can do. See you on Friday?' you say, tote bags in hand.

'Yeah, sis, I'll see you then,' he says. You're about to wave goodbye when he says, 'Oh and sis, I see you eyeing up my locs. We can talk about that too. I've got you.'

You laugh and then say, 'I would love that, man.'

He says goodbye and you do too. You begin your walk towards the downstairs car park, not realising that this seemingly small act of kindness will be the start of something beautiful for you both.

REGGIE CONTINUED

My mum called me on the Tuesday to tell me that Grandad had died. I was about to go into a client meeting when her name flashed on my phone. Like the time before, I knew. I knew this time though that he had passed, that his soul had departed the earth and that he was gone for good.

Two weeks later, it is a Wednesday and I am here again in Jamaica, months earlier than I anticipated. When I arrive after the long journey from Montego Bay to Mandeville, Grandad isn't on the veranda to greet me with a smile and melodic-sounding patois. A sadness spreads through me, but I do not cry.

The house is full but feels empty without him. Everyone is here. My mum, my aunt, my cousins and the extended family from Canada and various other segments of the diaspora. It is the first time everyone has been together in decades. Cars come down the driveway every few hours, and out pour brothers and sisters from Grandad's church. They send their condolences and stay for too long, expecting a cold drink and a plate of food. I wish they wouldn't. This was not how things were supposed to be. We should have been gathered like this to mark his ninety years of life. He only had four months left to his birthday.

I keep expecting Grandad to join those seated, to emerge from his car in his khaki cap, a soy patty in hand for me. But he doesn't. He is not here, but pieces of him are everywhere. His reading glasses rest on the mahogany cabinet in the front room. His weathered Bible, held together by masking tape, is in the spare room. Unopened tins of Heinz vegetable soup sit abandoned in the pantry cupboard. The news is on both at six o'clock and eight o'clock. He doesn't watch it. The untuned piano stands tall with a book of chorus on top that he doesn't play. Left in the cupboard is the green chipped mug, which he no longer drinks from.

But though he isn't here, I feel his presence. I feel his spirit, and I remember the baby within me. The baby within me that bears his name, who is now the size of a papaya. I have decided that I will bring him here as often as I can. That despite being a child of the fourth generation, a descendant of the Windrush warriors, he will remain connected to the soil. That he will know where he comes from. That he will know he carries the strength of his great-grandfather's name.

On the Thursday, my body hasn't yet adjusted to the time zone, so I drink fresh mint tea on the veranda before the rising of the sun. I sit for a while, listening to the sound of crickets and the whimpering of dogs in the distance. I manage to read only a few pages of this month's book club selection before I hear footsteps. They are my mother's. 'Hello, Sharn,' she says, kissing me on the head like she always did when I was a child. 'How are you feeling, my babes?'

I realise again that I hold such moments of tenderness close. A day after my last trip to Jamaica, hours before my call to David and minutes before my FaceTime to Niah, I drove to my childhood home. I greeted my mum at the front door with no speech, but tears that said more than a thousand words. Inside, she apologised and said that I was old enough to make my own decisions. I apologised too and said she had been right all along.

'Hey, Mum,' I say, feeling warm after her touch. 'I couldn't really sleep, to be honest, and I still feel pretty nauseous.'

She settles in the seat Grandad sat on during my last visit. 'That's normal. I had that for months when I was pregnant with you,' she says, a smile in her eyes. 'Try drinking some ginger tea tomorrow. That should help.'

'Ah yeah, I will try that,' I say, returning the smile. I remember that Grandad's medicinal tendencies run through her veins. And mine too.

We sit in silence for some time and then I ask her how she is doing. A tear falls from her eye. 'I know it sounds silly, but although he always spoke about dying, I always thought he would be here forever.' She stops. Her head is now cupped in her palms and I know that what she wants to say next is *I don't know what I'm going to do without him*. I take her hand and squeeze it tight, not knowing how I can ease her pain. She lifts her head and turns to me. 'He loved you so much, Sharna.'

The last time I was in Jamaica, Grandad told me that a child needs their mother. My own lost hers when she was eight years old. I think again of all she has lost. Of how much she has done for me. Of what she has sacrificed. 'I love you, Mum,' I say, the words sounding alien on my tongue.

I know she is surprised. I am not one generally to express affection so directly. But I am trying to be better at loving the people who I care about most whilst they are still here. I have seen over and over again the fragility of life, how things can change in an instance. There is gratitude in her eyes. She says, 'I love you too, my darling.'

Now I move closer to her in my chair, resting my head on her chest, feeling the gentle rise and fall of her breath. She places her hand on my face that is damp with sweat, her fingers running along my cheeks, lined with the small brown moles we both share. I close my eyes. I am glad I have my mother back. I will need a village to raise my son.

On the Friday, we awake to a wail. Aunty V cries tears from her depths. 'Finally,' my aunt says to my mum. 'She hasn't cried since he passed.'

We all gather around her, hands outstretched. She continues to howl. 'Oh Jesus, oh Jesus,' she sobs. She untangles herself from the hands that are holding her. She takes off her slippers and climbs onto the bed that her husband died in. She cries wet tears into the pillow for hours. I don't know what I can do to help.

The house carries a heaviness. Everyone has tears in their eyes, but still I haven't cried.

Later that day I take a seat under the pear tree. On my phone there is a message from Niah. *Keeping you in my thoughts and prayers sis. Let me know if there's anything you need. Love you.* I send three white heart emojis back and say *Love you too bestie.* Thinking about my secondary school English lessons with Niah and Ifey, I then take out my journal and I write for the first time in years.

I wish that you were still here. I wish that I could have spent more time with you. I miss you, but you will live on in me. You will live on in me through my green fingers. I will continue to remain connected to the soil, planting fresh produce in the garden like you taught me. You will live on in me when I am in the kitchen. Your recipes for rice and peas and rump steak are ones I will never forget.

I will continue to add a dollop of butter to steamed cabbage and will try my hand again at coconut cake, though it will never come close to yours. You will live on in me in the way that I handle my money. You always taught me to be a saver, to save for a rainy day. You will live on in me through my moments with the Creator. Though I have my doubts, I will pray like you always did. You will live on in me through my love for music. I will make sure that my son plays the piano, like Mum and in turn me. You will live on in me as I endeavour to do better in my friendships. To cherish and turn up for those who are closer than brothers in times of joy and in times of sorrow. You will live on in me through my gratitude for the gift of life. I promise to clap when I land every time your great-grandson and I come back to Jamaica.

Two nights before the day of the funeral, I am restless in bed because of the heat. When I finally manage to fall asleep, I have a dream. I dream that Grandad is dressed in a dark beige suit. His hair is not grey but jet black, and his face is free from wrinkles. I have seen this face before in black-and-white photographs of when he first came to England. He walks upright and there is no walking stick in sight. When he sees me, he places a swaddled bundle of white cloth in my arms. I wake up. I am not a modern-day Joseph. I do not know what the dream means.

I struggle to get back to sleep and so I get out of bed and walk to the kitchen. It is pitch-black. I walk in darkness. I am distracted by a fresh mosquito bite on my arm. And so I don't see the water that has leaked from the fridge onto the kitchen floor.

I slip.

There is blood. I hear myself scream, and then my vision blurs.

On the Sunday morning, I awake to walls I do not recognise. A drip is attached to my right arm. I realise that I am in a hospital. I am told by the doctor that what has happened is a miracle. That with a fall like the one I had, I should have lost the baby. My mum is by my side, my aunt's arms around her, both with tears in their eyes. 'Thank God,' she says. I hold my stomach. There is a gentle kick.

I close my eyes, and again I see the image of Grandad in a dark beige suit, his back strong. I remember the depth of his baritone, which filled the room when I last saw him with breath in his lungs. '*When peace like a river attendeth my way.*' I open my eyes, feel a lone tear fall. And then I am crying. My mum places her hand on my knee and she cries too. The sun is shining through the linen curtains. I smile with my whole mouth like Grandad and my mum. I take a deep breath and look up. I whisper, 'Thank you, Grandad. Thank you for your prayers that kept me, and now my son.'

THE THIRD DEATH

On the day her best friend's grandad died, Rianna realised she'd forgotten what her dad looked like.

I can't believe he's gone, Sharna had said earlier that morning in their group chat. And then the girls had sent their words of encouragement, together with love heart and sympathy emojis, and Rianna had too. But she'd felt some type of way. Her friend's grandad had lived to see his late eighties. He was warned of his death with time to prepare. And Sharna had spent two whole weeks with him in Jamaica, able to say goodbye. Once more, Rianna felt a creeping wave of something she had never experienced with her childhood friend: resentment. But also something else, something harder to define. She just couldn't recall her dad's face. She couldn't quite picture his features – his eyes, or the nose they shared. And she couldn't remember the distinct cadence of his voice or the rhythm of his slightly uneven walk.

Rianna stood up from the kitchen table of her flatshare and went up into her bedroom, closing the door firmly behind her. She took out her phone and scrolled to a photo album she'd titled ♡♡. Months after the funeral, Rianna's mum had removed all the pictures of her dad from the house. She said it was too painful to be reminded every day what she had lost. That the images intensified an inescapable sorrow of losing part of herself. But he had belonged to Rianna too.

She sat on her bed for some time, taking in the pictures, trying her best to commit them again to memory. She was thinking about the last phone call she'd had with her dad and the promise he'd made, when it came to her. She knew what she needed to do. She knew who she needed to see after all this time. She closed the album.

That morning, as usual, Vivienne was sitting in front of the TV, sipping her reheated tea. Her daily routine had remained unaltered for years: she would wake up, half-drink a cup of tea, shower, get dressed, attach her wig, watch daytime shows, eat dinner at 6 p.m., then retire to bed an hour later. Today was ordinary, but a significant date loomed just ahead. Despite her age, there were some moments she would never forget. She remembered her mother's birthday and the day she'd got married. She knew the exact date of when she'd arrived in England and the date she'd got divorced. She also remembered the day she'd lost her favourite son. It was a memory that weighed particularly heavily on her, etched into her soul. Benjamin's death had been the start of relentless grief – infighting in the family, the sudden descent of ailments on loved ones and then, sometime later, a pandemic. After the funeral she was different, overcome by low mood, with little energy for things that used to interest her. It was not the rightful order of things. A mother should not bury their child.

Vivienne's thoughts came to an abrupt halt. She paused the TV and shifted her weight towards the edge of the cushioned chair. She then made slow steps towards the cordless landline ringing in the hallway. She picked up the phone, put it to her ear and said, 'Hello.'

'Hi, Gran, it's me. Rianna.'

'Miss Flash!' said Vivienne. 'How are you doing?'

'Hi, Gran,' repeated her granddaughter with a slight laugh. 'I'm doing OK, just working from home today.'

'Good girl,' said Vivienne, walking slowly towards the armchair with a noticeable limp in her step.

'How are you? What are you up to?'

'I'm alright. Not doing much, girl. Just watching the news,' said Vivienne, lowering herself onto the seat again and tucking a blanket below her waist. 'So, tell me, how was that date you went on?' She was all too familiar with her granddaughter's experience of the dating app that was 'designed to be deleted'. She relished Rianna's stories about what she called the 'ghetto' of the dating world. She loved her analysis of the men she regarded as 'fuck boys' and her avoidance of what she referred to as 'red flags': disappearing without warning, lying about one's height, and not initiating dates.

'Meh, it was alright. The food was nice though,' said Rianna.

'Does this one have the cash then? The last one was so stingy, bloody cheek.'

'Oh, you still remember that guy?' said Rianna, laughing. 'God, that is still my worst date on record. He was a big, big lawyer but couldn't pay for a cheeky Nando's?'

'If you have to pay for your dinner, kick him to the kerb. I would have left him straight away, girl!' said Vivienne.

'Trust me, Gran, I haven't spoken to him since.' They both laughed hysterically. 'How are you though? When did you last go for a walk?'

Vivienne kissed her teeth. 'I can't be bothered. There's not much around here anyway.' She had once lived in a four-bedroom house in Tooting but now resided in a small bunga-low on the outer reaches of Surrey. She was no longer a few doors away from Sister Lewis from St Kitts, who would invite her over for black cake and tea with condensed milk every Tuesday. She had stopped going to the leisure centre on Thursdays for the women's-only swimming and sauna session. And it had been years now since she had attended the local church she was once part of for four decades.

'I hear that. But do you at least use the stick Uncle Leroy got you?' Rianna asked. Her eldest uncle had suggested the move. He said the absence of stairs would be good for Vivienne's limited mobility, given that she refused to have the hip replacement she needed. But everyone knew that he wanted his share of the money for the house that sat in the middle of a gentrified hotspot. She had given in. She had no more fight left in her.

'I don't want no damn stick. I'm fine,' Vivienne said, and kissed her teeth again. 'So tell me,' she continued, not giving Rianna time to respond. 'How is everything going?'

'I'm doing OK,' said Rianna. She stopped. 'Gran, I spoke to Sharna earlier. Her grandad died.'

Vivienne felt a tightness in her chest.

'I'm so sorry, Gran,' continued Rianna, filling the silence.

'It's alright, girl. It's how life goes,' said Vivienne. 'May he rest in peace. Reggie was a good man,' she continued, her voice trailing off.

'I know how close you all once were,' said Rianna.

'May they both rest in peace,' Vivienne said, just above a whisper.

'Sharna's going to Jamaica again for the funeral.'

'Thank God for that at least,' said Vivienne, attempting to mask the bitterness she felt. She had always imagined that she would be laid to rest on the east bank of the Demerara, close to those in her bloodline who had passed over before her. But here she was, still in the country she had once vowed she wouldn't die in.

'Gran?' said Rianna.

'Yes, girl?' Vivienne replied, adjusting the blanket to cover her feet.

'I wondered if . . .', Rianna hesitated. She started again. 'I wondered if I could come round and see you soon?'

Since lockdown, Vivienne hadn't taken well to having people in the house. She had grown accustomed to her children greeting her at the front door with a mask and maintaining a metre's distance between them. Despite the back and forth of social distancing rules, from support bubbles to the tiering system and then the eventual easing of restrictions, she still told everyone that they could come but that they weren't to stay too long.

'I can test before I come, if you want?' Rianna added.

Vivienne paused for a few seconds. Although she hadn't spoken to Rianna's mum since her son's funeral, Rianna was the only one of her twenty-seven grandchildren who called each week. She was the only grandchild who called at all. 'You could come for a little while. That would be OK,' she said.

'OK, great, thanks so much, Gran. I'll see you soon.'

'Good girl, good girl. Thanks for calling, right? OK then, bye, Rianna, bye bye,' Vivienne said.

Vivienne pressed the End Call button. She leaned forward, placing the house phone next to the empty mug on the wooden table in front of her. She looked at the glass cabinet opposite. It was home to crystal glasses and china only to be used on special occasions, with odd trinkets, royal family paraphernalia and various framed pictures of her children and grandchildren at graduation. She stood up and walked slowly towards the display case. On the bottom shelf was a rust-coloured photo album, slightly hidden. She pulled it out, causing dust to linger in the air. She settled on the adjacent brown sofa and opened the album.

The first photo showed her five daughters, Afros and brightly coloured attire in abundance, sitting on a brick wall. Beneath it was an image of family members dancing, with a cake and candles close by. She continued to turn the pages, the pictures not arranged in any chronological order: the whole family gathered at her nephew's wedding, everyone in shades of gold and champagne. The christening of her youngest grandson, all of her eight sons, sons-in-law and older grandsons posing, no one looking in the right direction. A square picture smaller than its see-through sleeve, showing a newborn baby, any one of her many grandchildren.

She continued to the next page and was met with a different time period, with photographs in black and white. Her great-grandmother on a wooden stool, a white handbag resting on her lap. Her four children born in Guyana clutching suitcases on the day they left for England.

She turned the page again. It was the picture she was looking for. Vivienne ran her fingers along its contours. She saw herself nearly sixty years younger, her face taut and mole-free, dressed in a tailored suit and a long winter coat, standing outside an old building. By her side was a woman, also in her mid twenties and dressed in a similar outfit, wearing a black hat decorated with lace. It was a cold November morning, days after her then-husband had sent for her, when Vivienne had first met her best friend, Millicent. Desperate for a piece of home and missing the children she had left behind, she had stumbled across a Pentecostal fellowship after being turned away from an Anglican denomination. Despite the lack of reverence for the sacraments – no breaking of bread or taking of wine, and the absence of stained-glass windows – she felt comfortable in the back of the rented school hall, with varying Caribbean accents and the familiar dropping of h's in speech. After that first service, she was welcomed by Millicent, who was also a nurse at St George's. She turned the page again. This time, the picture showed herself, her best friend and two other women, on the day the church bought their own building. They were all standing in a kitchen, dressed in plastic aprons with disposable hairnets covering their curls. 'Oh dear,' Vivienne said, laughing. 'Those were the days.'

The times of preparing food for the Tuesday lunch club and district conventions came to mind, with the exchange of recipes between islands and Vivienne teaching Millicent how to make roti and channa. She turned the page again. This time she saw Reggie in a pinstripe suit planting a kiss on Millicent's cheek, with a three-tier cake in view. She stared at the picture for some time, thinking about the many moments they had shared. Of cooking together, of singing in the church choir and of dropping off money for the Pardner after their shifts on a Thursday. Vivienne missed her best friend dearly. She looked again at Reggie and recalled how her love for Millicent had once coexisted with wishing her own husband was more like the man her friend had married. Hers had turned into something she had never expected – a stranger, violent and unfaithful.

Vivienne closed the album, kissed her teeth again and stood up to make her second cup of tea for the day.

Days later, on the anniversary of her dad's passing, Rianna arrived outside Vivienne's house. Though it had been some years now, she was still not used to the one-storeyed house with its sloping roof, though she had visited a handful of times. Rianna rang the doorbell and entered the porch.

There was the sound of locks unbolting before Vivienne emerged. 'Well I never, look at you, Miss Flash!' she said at the front door.

Vivienne looked different now, older. There were fine

lines around her eyes and mouth. Her posture was more stooped. But she still carried the same warm presence that made Rianna feel at ease. 'Hey, Gran,' Rianna said, reaching out for a hug. 'It's so good to see you.'

'You're looking skinny, girl. Have you been eating?' said Vivienne, withdrawing from the embrace.

Rianna laughed. 'I've been snacking way too much, being at home most of the week. I decided to take up running.'

'Don't lose too much weight now, you don't want to get too mauger. Come in, come in,' said Vivienne, ushering Rianna into the house.

Despite the exterior differences, the inside of Rianna's gran's house was an exact replica of her previous home in Tooting. The same mosaic of the Kaieteur Falls in a golden frame was by the front door and a banner with the words TOO BLESSED TO BE STRESSED hung above the shoe rack in the hallway. In the living room were the same brown sofas, covered in clear plastic, decorated with red and pink velvet cushions. Fake flowers still lined the shelves.

Taking off her shoes, Rianna caught sight of the record player in the corner of the front room. The living room had once been the hub for endless family gatherings with her thirteen aunties and uncles and countless cousins in attendance; with the sounds of soca and lovers' rock above the laughter of children running up and down the stairs. Her dad had once been able to mobilise the entire family, effortlessly bringing everyone together. But those days were no more. They hadn't gathered all together since his funeral over six years ago. It was the reason she hadn't visited her grandmother in years, deciding instead to call her. It was too painful to be reminded of how so much had changed.

'Do you want some tea?' said Vivienne, calling from the kitchen.

'Yes please, Gran. I'm coming.'

In the kitchen, the walls were the colour of cinnamon, fitted with wooden cupboards. On the granite worktop stood two microwaves, an orange jar labelled TEA, half a bottle of Vimto and a grey toaster with a matching kettle, just boiled. Rianna walked over to the empty mug by the kettle and reached for a teabag. She was pouring water into the mug when she noticed that Vivienne had placed half a cup of tea into the microwave.

'Why do you do that, Gran?' said Rianna, adding milk to her tea.

'Do what?' said Vivienne, not facing her.

'Put old tea in the microwave.'

'I can never drink a whole cup,' Vivienne replied.

'But why don't you just make a smaller amount or use a smaller mug?' asked Rianna, as she remembered her dad doing the same each morning.

'Habit, I guess,' Vivienne said.

Rianna watched as Vivienne walked towards the round wooden table, which was covered by a plastic tablecloth picturing Big Ben and a large red bus. Her grandmother moved more slowly than she remembered, each step a conscious manoeuvre, the bend in her back more accentuated.

'So tell me, how was the date?' said Vivienne, settling into a chair.

Rianna had noticed over the years that her grandmother would repeat things, forgetting conversations they'd already had. 'Mmm, it was alright. The food was good,' she said, taking a seat opposite Vivienne. She stopped. 'He did say something that rattled me, though.'

'Go on,' said Vivienne, leaning further into her seat.

'So, we were having a decent conversation and then he was like, "You're half Guyanese, right? Can you make roti?"'

'What a damn cheek,' said Vivienne.

'I know, right?' said Rianna. But what she didn't mention to her grandmother was how this date had made her think of her dad's promise the day before he died: that he would finally show her how to make roti.

'Don't mind him anyway,' said Vivienne, taking a sip of her tea. 'What a cheek.'

'I know, Gran.'

On her way home after the date, Rianna had tried to calm herself down with gratitude: grateful that she'd had such a wonderful father for twenty-one years of her life; that it was better to have loved and lost than never to have loved at all. But then she thought of all the moments she

did not get to enjoy: her dad seeing her graduate, him helping with the DIY at her flat and cheering her on as she
received an 'upcoming engineers to watch' award. And
then there were all the moments she would never have: her
dad walking her down the aisle, and him holding her first
child.

'These men, I tell you. What a waste of space,' continued
Vivienne. 'All they want is your food, your sex, and to make
you have a whole heap of children.'

Rianna smiled at the phrase her grandmother had used
many times before. She then gently cupped the mug in
her hand. 'But his comment did get me thinking . . .' She
stopped. 'I know you said you don't cook like that any
more, but I wondered if you could just talk me through
the steps?'

'You have some nerve, you,' said Vivienne, chuckling.

Rianna took another sip of her tea and looked at the
weathered wooden plate in front of her. At its centre was an
irregular rectangular land mass, surrounded by a water lily,
a cathedral and a bird with a feathered crest. It dawned on
her again, as it had the evening after her last date, that she
didn't know anything about the land of her father. That bar
waving both the St Lucian and Guyanese flags at carnival,
she didn't know anything about the country that claimed
half of her. On the train home following her date, she'd
googled facts about Guyana. But finding out that it was the
only English-speaking nation in South America, or that its

national bird was the hoatzin, seemed irrelevant. And she had been met with a loss of a different kind, realising she couldn't research her way into a piece of her identity she felt was missing.

'Please, Gran,' said Rianna, putting down her mug. 'You know Dad loved it, and you could just tell me what to do and I could make note of the steps,' she said, taking out her phone. 'Please,' she said again, meeting Vivienne's gaze. 'I need this.'

Vivienne looked at Rianna for a few moments, then said, 'I don't have any plain flour.' She placed her mug on the ceramic coaster. 'You'll need to go to the corner shop and get some, right?'

Minutes after Rianna left the house, Vivienne walked over to the cupboard and took out a wooden rolling pin and a dulled cast iron tawa. She filled a measuring jug with water and took out a bottle of vegetable oil from the cupboard above the stove. After placing a container of salt on the table, she settled back into her chair. She remembered the depth of longing in her granddaughter's eyes moments before. She saw Benjamin in Rianna. He was the only one of her children who had seen cooking not only as a necessity but as a creative act, like she had once done. She'd taught him everything he knew. She stood up and made another cup of tea.

'Right, you,' said Vivienne, half an hour after Rianna had returned with a bag of flour in a blue plastic bag. 'I've never used recipe books or any nonsense like that. It's best if you just watch me. That's how my mother taught me, and her mother before that.' She opened up the packet of plain flour and poured half its contents into a large bowl. She next added one and a half teaspoons of baking powder and poured some salt into the bowl.

'How much salt did you use, Gran?' asked Rianna.

'Girl, I don't know about measurements, I just know about eyeing. With practice you just sort of know,' said Vivienne. She poured water into the mixture and began stirring it together with a wooden spoon.

'I see,' said Rianna, typing frantic notes on her phone.

Vivienne began to knead the mixture together with her right hand, periodically adding more flour. With every back and forth motion, the beige dough became softer. 'I haven't made roti in a very long time, girl,' said Vivienne after a few moments of silence. Years before, at Christmas and over Easter, her old kitchen would be filled with an array of dishes: cook-up rice, garlic pork, dhal, channa, chow mein and rotis stacked high on greaseproof paper. Benjamin had once moved between being DJ in the living room and helping her in the kitchen.

'Why's that, Gran?' asked Rianna.

'It's too much damn effort,' said Vivienne as she picked up the dough and passed it from one hand to the other.

'Fair enough,' said Rianna. She watched her grand-mother continue to move the dough between her hands.

'Dad once told me that you were going to open a restaurant in Guyana,' said Rianna, her voice trailing off.

A lifetime ago, Vivienne had been one of the best cooks in Georgetown, with people coming from far and wide to taste her roti. Her ex-husband said that they would return after five years of working and building up their savings in the UK so she could open Vivienne's Kitchen. But five years in England turned into six, six years into ten, and ten into sixty-one. And Vivienne went from having three sons and two daughters to having thirteen children, twenty-seven grandchildren, eight great-grandchildren and then a divorce. 'Yes, girl,' she said, rolling the dough into a ball. A quiet settled between them once more.

'Did you ever want to go back, Gran?'

Vivienne looked over at the white fridge covered in plastic fruit magnets. 'It's too damn hot. And the mosquitoes, they're too much of a headache,' she said eventually.

And it was true. The heat was unbearable at times, and she was no longer used to the tropical insects. When she had returned for a holiday after leaving over fifty years ago, with her then-husband and the few children who considered themselves Guyanese, it had felt different.

'It's not the same,' she continued. 'Once you leave and come back, people treat you differently. They think you have more money, more cash, you speak a bit different . . . It's too much trouble.'

'I hear that,' said Rianna. 'What about the restaurant

though?' Did you ever think about starting up anything here?'

Vivienne picked up a tea towel from the kitchen counter before placing it over the bowl. Benjamin had once suggested something similar. One day, between dipping layers of roti into a plate of chicken curry, he'd said that Vivienne's Kitchen would be a hit in South London. He saw something in her beyond being a bearer of children and the ex-wife of a serial cheater. Their chats and the potential of a family restaurant had ended when she had received the call from Rianna's mother. Her son had had a heart attack in the shower, dying aged fifty-one.

'No, not really. It would be too much work,' said Vivienne. She sat down again. 'Do you want some more tea?'

'Nah, I'm good thanks, Gran.'

'What about a piece of cake? I have some madeira,' said Vivienne.

'I'm alright, thanks.'

Another pause hung in the air.

'Gran,' said Rianna.

'Yes, girl.'

'I'm forgetting,' said Rianna, not looking at her grandmother.

'What do you mean?' said Vivienne.

'I'm forgetting what he looked like,' said Rianna, as she met Vivienne's gaze.

Vivienne knew of the terror of this third death – not the failure of body, or no longer feeling someone's presence, but their face fading from memory. She placed her hand on Rianna's shoulder and her tears began to fall. As her granddaughter was reaching for a packet of tissues in her bag, Vivienne stood up and left the kitchen.

When she returned, she had a weathered photo album in her hands. She opened it, turning to the middle of the large book, and passed it to Rianna. 'Here.'

Rianna looked at a photo of her dad with more hair on his head than she'd ever seen. He looked no more than three years old and was barefoot, dressed in a cotton shirt with matching shorts. Behind him was a cluster of fishing boats, and he was holding a large, shiny fish. 'I've never seen this before,' said Rianna, her eyes glistening with tears. 'This is in Mahaica, right?'

'Yes,' said Vivienne, her eyes following the river that flowed into the Atlantic Ocean.

Rianna continued to turn the pages, seeing pictures of her dad and his older siblings in their formative years, with bodies of water and dense vegetation as a backdrop. She saw images of places she'd never seen before – a large clock tower, a bustling market filled with merchants, and vast rice fields.

The next picture looked out of place. It was a smaller sepia photograph, with Vivienne in a high-necked white dress, her hair in loose pressed curls. Holding her hand was the man who had moved to America with his new wife and family several years before Rianna was born. He was the man who no one spoke about but whom, she now saw, bore an uncanny resemblance to her dad.

Vivienne shifted in her seat and took a sip of her tea. Rianna turned the page again and this time saw her dad a few years older, in a grey suit too big for him, standing next to some of her aunties and uncles with an airport terminal in the background. She looked at it for some time.

'Your father nearly died earlier that day,' said Vivienne.

'He almost drowned, right?' said Rianna, not looking at her grandmother. The near-fatal accident was the reason her dad had insisted on Rianna having swimming lessons from the age of four. It was the reason she was in the fifth year of running her social enterprise, passionate about water safety and aquatic sports amongst ethnic minorities.

'He did. He jumped into the trench. He thought that if he got his suit wet he wouldn't be able to leave for England. He wanted to stay with his friends,' said Vivienne, with a faint laugh.

'No way? He never told me that part,' said Rianna. She turned the page again. This time she saw her dad as an adult, not yet bald but with a Jheri curl. His arms were wrapped around her mum, her belly with a noticeable bump. She smiled. 'She used to be so happy,' said Rianna, as she turned to another picture of her parents on their wedding day. Her childhood home had once carried the warmth of two people deeply in love.

On the next page was an image of the whole family at the celebration for her grandmother's seventy-fifth birthday. She zoned in on her father, who was standing in the far right-hand corner. 'I miss him. He was the glue that kept us all together,' she said. After her dad's sudden death, the family had spiralled into chaos, lacking leadership. Next came the arguments over money and the funeral arrangements. And then, after he was laid to rest, her mum had cut all ties with her dad's side of the family.

Rianna came to the end of the album. 'I wish we'd more time,' she said.

'I know,' said Vivienne. 'I know, girl.'

Rianna closed the book and placed it on the table.

'You can keep it,' said Vivienne.

'You sure, Gran?'

'Yes, my girl. My eyes aren't what they used to be anyway.'

'Thanks so much, Gran,' said Rianna. 'I'll keep it safe.'

Vivienne stood up and removed the tea towel from the bowl. She picked up a sharp knife and cut the dough into six equal parts before rolling the sections into small balls.

As Rianna watched Vivienne flattening the pieces of dough with a rolling pin, it occurred to her that she would not be here if her dad hadn't survived the drowning when he was a child. She wondered how life would be if he hadn't come to England. If he hadn't studied at university and developed an interest in local politics. If he hadn't attended the Black Labour Caucus meeting in Wandsworth Town

Hall one evening. If he hadn't been seated next to the stranger who would later become his wife. As her grandmother flipped over the portions of dough, repeating the motion, Rianna thought further back, to other decisions that were also out of her control but had formed the tapestry of her life: the call from the mother country to the colonies, her grandad moving to London and Vivienne joining him a year later. Her grandmother meeting Sharna's grandmother at church. Her and Sharna attending the same nursery, inseparable. Years later, her childhood friend moving to the other side of South London and introducing Rianna to some of her friends at a games night. Their now active group chat. Rianna, soon to be a godmother to her first godchild. She was suddenly emotional, filled with gratitude for her dad's life, for her life, for her friendships, and for this very moment.

Using a small pastry brush, Vivienne added a mix of vegetable oil and shortening to the flattened balls of dough and put down the rolling pin, sprinkled flour onto each piece and said, 'Try to look at the pictures as often as you can. That's how you will keep him alive.'

Rianna turned to her grandmother and said, 'I will, Gran.'

'Good girl, good girl,' said Vivienne, before walking over to the hob and adding oil to the tawa. Rianna stood up to join her. Vivienne placed the first piece of circular flattened dough into the pan and Rianna thought of all that her grandmother had loved and lost: her country, her dream, her childhood love, her closest friends, and her son.

Rianna turned to Vivienne again and said 'Gran, have you ever been on a staycation?'

'A stay-what?' said Vivienne.

Rianna laughed. 'A staycation,' she repeated. 'It's a break somewhere in the UK.'

'Why would I want to do that? I can just stay in my own damn house, girl,' said Vivienne.

'I was thinking that it could be nice. And anyway, you could do with a change of scenery.'

Vivienne flipped over the dough with her bare hands, and passed Rianna a fish slice.

'I could pick you up, book a nice hotel somewhere with a spa so you can swim. What do you reckon?' said Rianna. Her dad had once said that she was nomadic in nature, like her grandmother had been. That as a teenager, Vivienne had taken the ferry to neighbouring Suriname, and after her divorce had taken solo trips to Spain, Greece, and even to Canada to visit her sister.

'I guess it could be nice. But not too far now. I know how you love to stray and go off to these far, far foreign places,' said Vivienne, laughing.

Rianna watched the dough slowly turn to a darker beige, now fluffy with brown spots. 'Yes, I think it could be, Gran. It would be lovely,' said Rianna and smiled.

BACK TO THE OFFICE

When the lift arrives on the fourth floor, it's like nothing has changed. But I've forgotten how to navigate the building.

It feels like an eternity as I walk up and down, struggling to find my locker. It's been so long, I can't recall where it is. I pace the empty corridors, my feet still on some sort of autopilot. Finally, I stumble across the right block of white plastic compartments. I put my key into the wrong locker, twice. On my third attempt, the key turns. The patent tassel loafers I couldn't find this morning fall out. There is a canvas bag full of paper from a training course I did days before we were told to take all our belongings and laptops home. There are pens, a wireless keyboard and a presentation clicker that I forgot to return to IT. I move some items around, then I stuff my coat and scarf inside.

I make my way to my allocated 'hot desk' for the day. I have not missed being here, in an environment that demands that you be ultra-visible: arriving early and staying late, socialising with colleagues in your own time, and answering emails outside of working hours to climb to the top. I pass a collaboration area, a space to which I regularly escaped to avoid the constant office chatter and to get work done. I remember the continual performance, and the morph into a being that isn't naturally me, despite being urged to 'bring my whole self to work'. I could have easily done today's meetings from my bed with my camera off or sat at the makeshift desk in my kitchen. I would much rather be at home in unironed joggers and an oversized T-shirt, with no bra on. But, for the first time in two years, I have on a blouse, a blazer and tailored chinos that are now tight around my waist.

A small Christmas tree is propped up on a table. It was already gathering dust in the March before everything changed, and it still hasn't been taken down. To my left is a whiteboard mounted on the wall. A list of key events, over a six-month period, are written in black permanent marker. The words *Events for 2020* are underlined in red ink. I walk around the corner, remembering that the office, for the most part, is synonymous with a constant feeling of anxiety. As rain pours from the sky outside, I pass the women's toilets. Once a place of solace for me and my girls, I now feel a sting of sadness. Those who made coming to work a little more bearable are no longer here. Niah left nearly two years ago now, moving to a different industry after the chaos following the interview for her diversity and inclusion role. Then Dami was headhunted for a role she could not refuse: twice her previous salary and with regular opportunities for travel.

One of the cleaners walks out, pushing a trolley stocked with toilet roll and cleaning products. She smiles, and I smile too. Though I've forgotten her name, I am grateful for this one element of work that has remained the same despite the changes that surround me.

'Hi, Mima,' says my manager as I enter the room for our 9 a.m. team meeting. Though this is the first time seeing her in the flesh, I feel as though I know her. But there is an awkwardness behind the smiles. We aren't friends, therefore a hug doesn't seem appropriate, but a handshake seems too formal.

'You're a lot taller than I thought you would be, Mima,' declares another colleague who arrives just after me, who I see for the first time as a full body and not a face on a screen. Other members of my team trickle in. They all mention that they are happy to be back. They welcome the new hybrid working policy of being in the office two days a week. They say that they have missed the social interaction, the moments spent in the kitchen making coffees, and the work drinks at the pub after five. I, on the other hand, have become accustomed to keeping my day job as small as possible, making space in my life for the things that bring me joy. I'd got used to listening to Tems on full blast between meetings and watching live music sets on YouTube whilst frying eggs to have with toast during my lunch break. I haven't missed the comments about my change of hairstyle, or people mistaking me for a more junior colleague who looks nothing like me. I force a smile.

After a morning of back-to-back meetings, some virtual and some in person, it's finally lunchtime. I join the queue for hot food. In the times before, I would have brought something in and heated it in the nearby microwaves. But the concept of meal prep is now alien. After paying for my tuna pasta bake with a side of salad, I take a seat at a table too big for me. I miss my girls. Five years ago, we met in the bathroom on the fourth floor. I had just come out of the cubicle when a woman I had never seen before smiled, said she liked my crochet braids and told me her name was Niah. After washing our hands, we walked out together and saw Dami, who looked a similar age to us. That was the beginning of our group chat, our Black women's book club and our lunches together most days in the canteen. I pick up my phone. I type: *It's so weird being back in the office. Even weirder without you guys here* 😞

There isn't a response.

I then message the wider group chat of Black colleagues that Niah, being a social butterfly, created years ago. She had made it her mission to greet every young Black person in the building and invite them to lunch on a Thursday. It was an hour filled with joy and laughter that made the instances of corporate microaggressions a little easier. They were moments we all yearned for. We needed each other, and it was our safe space. A space where we could be our whole selves without fear of ridicule, a place where we championed each other and shared opportunities both personal and professional. It was a place where we laughed. And then years later our conversations extended to discussions about the changes that Covid had brought into our lives and the nightmare of navigating Black Lives Matter virtually but still working. Through the exhaustion we supported each other with messages, voice notes and memes. But now the group chat is mostly inactive. Many have moved on, realising there is more money to be made elsewhere. Others needed something new.

Again, there is no response.

I open up YouTube, put in my AirPods and try to suppress my loneliness.

Someone is speaking to me, but I can't hear them. I take out an earphone. 'Do you mind if I sit here?' he says.

I look up. There is a man standing by the seat opposite me. I have never seen him in the building before. He is tall, clean-shaven and has a fresh trim with a taper fade. His skin glistens under the fluorescent lights of the canteen. I pause Koffee's Tiny Desk and say, 'No, go ahead,' though I notice there are a number of empty tables surrounding us. I suddenly feel anxious.

'Cool, thanks,' he replies as he sits down. His words are only two syllables, but I hear the thickness of his vocal cords, wrapped in a warm confidence. He wears a light blue cotton shirt that sits snugly around his biceps and a pair of brown semi-rimmed glasses that frame his face. I realise he has ordered the same meal as me.

He clocks this too, so after he pulls in his chair he adds, 'How is it?'

'Meh, I've had worse,' I reply, putting down my fork, the anxiety slowly fading. I could stop there, but I don't. I take out the remaining earphone and place it on the table. 'Not as bad as the rice and peas they tried to make one Black History Month.'

'God, did it have garden peas in it?' he asks.

'It did.' I laugh. 'How did you know?'

'I hear it. They did something similar at my old company. What an awful, awful day,' he laments.

We burst into laughter. For some reason I feel comfortable. I channel my inner Niah, my natural introversion falling away, and I say, 'So, you're new here?'

He tells me that he joined during lockdown and that this is his first time in the office. We fall into an easy conversation, which is unusual for me. I tell him I have worked here for a while, but that this is my first day back since the implementation of the new policy. Between mouthfuls of pasta, we talk about where we live and where we studied at university, which we agree feels like many moons ago. We realise we have mutual friends.

'Such a small world,' he says. 'Were you in the ACS too?' he continues, taking a sip of water. I am distracted by the beauty mark on his right hand. It is a mirror to the one on my left hand. A supposed sign of talent or intelligence. I wonder what it means for him.

'I wasn't on the committee. But I lived with everyone that was, so I was basically part of the team,' I say, my gaze returning to the pools of bronze in his eyes.

'An honorary member, like me,' he smiles, perhaps recalling fond memories from the African-Caribbean Society at university. 'The good days before the rat race.'

'For real! Before the realities of adulting,' I respond, before taking my final mouthful of pasta.

There is silence for a split second, but it isn't awkward. Rather, it is an acknowledgement of the moment of reflection, like a comma in a sentence and not a full stop. I take him in. He has a scar below his left eyebrow. I want to know the story behind the textured mark. I want to know if he fell off his bike when he was in primary school or if the story is more sinister. Maybe he notices me staring, because he looks at the paused video and says, 'So, you're a fan of Koffee too.'

'I have literally watched this video a thousand times,' I confess, delight spreading through me. 'It's just such good vibes. Real joy.'

He smiles and a dimple appears on his right cheek. I have the sudden urge to put my finger in the dip. I want to know how deep it is. I wonder if he is ticklish.

'Yeah man, and Tiny Desks are life. Do you have a favourite?'

I feel him looking at me, focusing on me alone. Like it's just me and him together in the canteen, with no one else around. I'm slightly flustered, but I manage to blurt out, 'I love, love H.E.R.'s one.' I forget my train of thought. 'Yeah, she is everything. So mad talented.'

'H.E.R. is levels for real,' he says, pulling his chair even further in.

'Right? Do you play any instruments?' I ask, realising I want to know everything about him.

'I play the keys actually,' he reveals, and there is a sudden spark in his eyes.

'Snap, me too,' I say, elated. 'Well, sort of. I've been on a seven-year sabbatical.'

He laughs. 'A seven-year sabbatical, yeah?'

I move my plate to the side. 'I wanted to focus all of my energies on one instrument. The guitar is my first love. Oh, and singing and songwriting, I'm really trying to get in my bag with that.'

He leans further into his chair. I feel his intense gaze. 'A talented woman. I love that.'

A surge of heat rushes through me. 'What sorts of things do you play?' I say, needing to avert his attention from me.

'I'm actually in a group, well a collective of musicians. I play the keys, we have a bassist, a drummer and a guitarist. We describe it as jazz fusion.' He stops. 'Think Snarky Puppy meets Robert Glasper.'

A dream, I scream on the inside, but thankfully the words don't materialise aloud. 'It sounds amazing. Is your stuff online?' I ask.

He takes out his phone and gets up. He settles on the seat next to me, which takes me by surprise. 'This is from the last show we did in person,' he says, opening a video from his camera roll. His arm brushes mine as he passes me one of his AirPods to put into my ear.

He presses play. All of a sudden, I am no longer back in the office with colleagues I would rather see on the screen. I forget that my girls have now left and it's just me, at work, by myself. Instead, I am transported into an underground venue with blue mood lighting. There is the smell of spilled alcohol, must and cigarettes. I am surrounded by tote bags and beards in need of shaving. Drinks are in hand. He is the first to come to the stage and takes a seat at a red Nord keyboard. A spotlight shines on glistening brown skin against black and white. I see the joy in his eyes as he plays a mix of dominant sevenths and augmented fourths in extended chords, with the odd collection of chromatic grace notes stirred in. His head bops slowly from side to side and there is a scrunching in his lips. At times he closes his eyes, feeling the music in the depths of his soul. I know the feeling. I feel it when my fingers brush against the strings of my guitar and a melody flows from my lips. The sounds he creates with his beauty-marked hands make me want to lift my hands in worship. To praise not God or a man who people call Saviour, but the music itself. He looks at me looking at him on the screen, and he smiles. Everything else falls away. I could live in this moment forever. It's just me, him and the music.

My work phone pings.

I am thrust back into reality. 'Damn, I have a meeting at two.'

He pauses the video and looks at his Apple Watch. 'Mad, same.'

We get up from the table and take our plates and trays to the bin area. As he scrapes away his food, I say, 'That was incredible,' my words feeling inadequate.

He faces me. 'Thank you. It's my happy place.'

I want to be in your happy place, I wish I could whisper. Instead, I smile and say, 'I can tell.'

Together we leave the canteen, and we talk about how much we have missed live music events over the last few years. 'Insta Live was great, but it did not hit in the same way at all,' he says.

'Right? I missed Troy Bar so much,' I reply, reminiscing on my favourite open mic night in Shoreditch.

'You know about Troy Bar, yeah?' he chuckles as we approach the lifts.

'Do *I* know about Troy Bar?' I remark, aghast. 'My big brother started taking me there ages ago – way before I was old enough to go, now I think about it.' I use his phrase, 'It's *my* happy place.'

He looks at me and smiles with his eyes. Before he gets a chance to reply, the lift arrives and we make our way inside. He presses the button for the third floor and asks, 'What floor do you work on?'

'I'm on the fourth floor,' I reply, but I want him to ask something more so we can stay in this moment a little longer. I've never been one to make the first move, but it's as though we've already gone past that. It's just me, him and a silence draped in limitless possibility. Before I go against everything I believe in and shoot my shot, he turns to me.

'I'm actually going to a gig tonight in Deptford. One of the guys from the band is playing.' He pauses. 'Would you want to come?' He stops again. 'I mean, if you're free?'

My brain scans a list of responses. I don't want to appear overly keen, but I want him to know I am interested. I want to play it cool. I fail. 'I would love to come,' I say, the 'o' in love elongated.

The lift approaches the third floor. Again, he looks at me, a longing in his eyes. Inside, I am melting. The doors open. 'I'll IM you with the details,' he says.

'Perfect,' I reply, as he steps out of the lifts. 'Wait,' I exclaim at a volume that is a lot louder than I would have hoped.

He turns to face me. 'Wow. We've been talking all of this time and I didn't even get your name,' he says, reading my thoughts.

Someone outside the lift makes their way inside. The doors begin to close. The man who I have bared my soul to in less than an hour blocks them.

'Mima,' I answer, 'Mima Mushana.'

'Mima Mushana,' he mouths, repeating my name like a song. I have never heard my name sound so beautiful. I can hear its meaning in Shona, the words combined: a dove, basked in sunshine. Before the doors close, I hear him say, 'I'm Tafari. Tafari Kassa.'

As the lift approaches the fourth floor, I take out my phone from my pocket. A text from Niah on iMessage reads: *Ah I can imagine, miss you xx*

Dami has typed, *How's it been going in girl?*

I exhale, and then I smile. I type: *It's actually been alright. Not me meeting the most amazing man in the canteen?!*

Outside it has stopped raining, and the sun is trying to break through.

OUTRO: THE GATHERING

The smells of curry goat and jerk chicken fill the house.

Rice and peas, mixed with creamed coconut, garnished with fresh thyme and scallion, bubble in a weathered Le Creuset pot in the kitchen. There are sputters of oil on mosaic tiles from the stirring of red peppers, ackee and saltfish and the deep-frying of festivals. A green banana and plantain curry for those with vegetarian and vegan leanings simmers in a small saucepan. The mac and cheese in the oven below is near golden and crispy. In the room next to the kitchen, which has come to be known as the Orange Room because of the deep satsuma walls, is an array of snacks: sweets, popcorn and crisps on a large wooden table covered with a beige tablecloth. Bottles of alcoholic beverages and soft drinks are poised on a side table. Rose gold and metallic pearl confetti balloons are scattered on the floor. There is a matching banner plastered to the wall that reads HAPPY BIRTHDAY. Under soft mood lighting and lit tea lights, neo soul sounds through a large speaker in the hallway. For the first time in a long time, the house is full of laughter and rows of shoes by the front door.

Niah, Gabby and Ifey are gathered in the kitchen. It has been a while since they have all been together like this. They recount memories from over a decade ago, and how these gatherings, hosted by Niah since they were seventeen and in sixth form, have been missed recently. They muse on how the attendees have evolved over the years. They laugh about how much has changed: locations, jobs and relationship status, and about what has remained the same.

Mima and Dami are seated in the Orange Room, red cups in hand. They have never been to one of Niah's annual events and so they gape at the double bass that stands in the corner and the many, many books on the shelves opposite. By the piano sit Tafari and Michael, who try to figure out how they know each other, whether it's from an initiative for Black students or a summer internship during university. 'I dunno, I feel like it could be both,' says Tafari. 'Nice to meet you though,' says Michael. 'It seems like Niah is very bait anyway.'

The doorbell rings. Niah leaves the kitchen and opens the front door. Rianna enters, with a bag of roti in hand that is still warm. 'I made some again today with my gran,' she says, before taking off her shoes and putting on the house slippers that come out of her bag. Moments later, Tariq enters with a bottle of Prosecco, giving Ifey a kiss on the cheek. 'What are you doing here?' he says, elated, as he stands by the front room door and sees Khari seated with Jada, Niecey and Destiny. Shortly afterwards, Emmanuel arrives with David, who makes a grand entrance with a bottle of Cîroc in hand. He sees the birthday girl in the kitchen and says, 'We getting lit tonight?' Everyone laughs and Niah says, 'It's not everyday Dubai enjoyment, David.'

Sharna comes downstairs after showering and changing out of the house clothes she had worn whilst helping Niah prepare the food for today's function. 'You look cute, Mama,' says Niah, looking at the swelled bump beneath her maxi dress. 'Not as cute as you, birthday girl,' says Sharna, returning the compliment. As co-host for the evening, she walks into each room and greets everyone, before re-entering the kitchen to stir the rice that has finished cooking and to reheat the pots on the stove. There is a steady pouring in of people as the sky outside darkens. Joy permeates every room.

The music is lowered; it is time to eat. With Gabby's help, Ifey has put the food into an assortment of large serving bowls and has brought everything through into the Orange Room. It is a feast.

Jonathan has arrived and catches sight of Gabby in the kitchen. He's barely taken off his coat when he sees David, and before he even says hello he is laughing. They embrace, and Black Boy Joy fills the air. Niah sees the interaction and asks Jonathan to bless the food. 'Man hasn't even taken off his shoes yet,' he replies. There is laughter. Everyone bows their heads, and Jonathan gives thanks for the food, for fellowship, and Niah's twenty-eight years of life. After a reverberation of amens and clapped hands, the music plays again through the speaker. With paper plates and plastic cutlery in hand, an informal queue forms. Plates are stacked high with food, and every-one settles in a seat or stands.

Conversations continue between mouthfuls of food. Some return to the table for a second and third plate. Red cups are topped up with beverages from the drinks table, which is now overflowing. In the front room, there is commotion mixed with belly laughter. Emmanuel, the gamemaster for the night, has divided those seated into two teams for a game of Articulate. Everyone is competitive, with differing views on the rules. Khari has left Niecey and Destiny and is sitting at the bottom of the stairs talking to Rianna.

Just after eleven, the music comes down and everyone gathers again in the Orange Room. Sharna enters with a birthday cake and there are candles. Mima starts to sing 'Happy Birthday', the Stevie Wonder version, and every-one joins in. There is a gentle alto harmony amongst the singers of the group. After Niah blows out the candles with a waving of her hands, she smiles. Everyone claps. 'Speech, speech,' shouts David. There is laughter.

'I actually wanted to make a toast,' says Niah, handing the cake to Sharna. 'Guys, thank you all so much for coming. It's so great to see you all like this after so long,' she continues. There are smiles, there are nods. 'It's not just a time to celebrate me, but us all. Mate, what a year it has been. Two years even.' Niah raises a glass of moscato that has been handed to her by Jada. 'To us all,' she says. 'It's been one hell of a few years, but we made it. Some didn't. So here's to life and new life,' she says, turning to Sharna and raising her glass. At seven months pregnant, Sharna looks down at her belly in acknowledgement. David, who is standing at the back, inhales and feels the firm hand of Jonathan on his shoulder. Gabby looks at Jonathan and then looks away. There is a clinking of glasses, and the word 'cheers' echoes through the room.

Rianna and Gabby take the cake back into the kitchen and cut it up into small slices, which are wrapped in kitchen towel and handed out to everyone who wants a piece. In the front room, Emmanuel starts a second round of Articulate, before a game of Mafia. In the Orange Room, Tafari dabbles on the piano, his own rendition of 'Happy' by Pharrell Williams, with the key signature changed. Everyone nods along, but few realise what the song is, thinking it is an original. He then plays what everyone recognises as 'Toast' by Koffee, and Mima smiles. There is dancing, and reggae beats and gratitude fill the air.

Shortly before midnight, the doorbell rings. Niah, who is in the hallway, walks over to open it. It's Tariq's friend, who was in the area. She welcomes him in and introduces him to those gathered in the kitchen. As he is talking to Tariq, she realises he looks familiar. She's sure she has met him before but she can't recall where. Back in the hallway, she offers him a drink and together they walk into the Orange Room. After he has thanked her for the uncorked bottle of Supermalt, he catches sight of the bookshelf. He takes a few steps forward and picks up *Homegoing* by Yaa Gyasi. 'This is one of my all-time favourites,' he says. And then it comes to Niah. He is the man from the train. The man who was reading her favourite book. The man who she never saw again. She smiles softly and says, 'It's mine too.'

It is after 2 a.m. when the food is done, any extra carted off in Tupperware containers for those who wanted more. Tafari has finished facilitating a vibrant round of karaoke and Emmanuel has concluded a second round of blackjack. Khari has asked Rianna for her number and Jonathan has decided against speaking to Gabby. The man who was reading Niah's favourite book says it would be nice to see her again.

After all of this, there is a steady exodus as everyone rubs their eyes and puts on their shoes. Some order Ubers, others locate their car keys and offer lifts to those who came on public transport. The mound of coats and jackets that has formed on the bannister in the hallway diminishes as people wave and say their goodbyes.

'Love you, sis,' says David, one of the last to leave. 'I needed tonight.' He opens the door and he and Jonathan begin their walk towards their cars.

After everyone has gone and after the plates of leftover food and empty red cups have been thrown away, the balloons popped and the HAPPY BIRTHDAY banner taken down, Niah and Sharna settle on the sofa with a glass of non-alcoholic wine in hand and share a piece of birthday cake.

'Thanks for all of your help, babe. I had such a great time,' says Niah.

'Of course. I've always got you, girl. And we needed this, it's been so long.'

Their glasses clink. 'Here's to living, baby girl,' says Niah. She puts a hand on Sharna's belly and says, 'Here's to living, baby boy.'

ACKNOWLEDGEMENTS

First and foremost, all glory to the Author of Life. I am thankful to God for giving me the strength, courage, discipline, inspiration and creativity to write these stories and for blessing me with the gift of writing. It's been a journey of resilience and faith and I am so grateful for His faithfulness in seeing me through.

Thank you to my parents, David and Pauline, for your unending love and encouragement. Thank you for instilling in me a passion for words through reading with me as a child, trips to the library, and for the many many books you bought me from before I could talk, through to my adult years. Thank you for the safe space of our home, for the countless family dinners and debates in the Orange Room, and for reminding me that I could be anything I wanted to be. Thank you for teaching me to speak up and to use my voice. This book exists because of you both.

To my family and village, Sheeda, Rachel, Kemi, Samara, James, Julien, Aunty Judy, Aunty Ola, Mya, Saf and the babies dem – Reya-Nyomi, Jos, Nate, Solly and Torah, thank you for your continued support not just for this book but for everything I do. I love you with my whole heart and I wouldn't be me without you all. Thank you also to my grandparents, all of the extended family and my family friends; I appreciate you all.

To my incredible agent, Sian Ellis-Martin, we did it, Joe! Thank you so much for taking a chance on me, and for signing me when my manuscript wasn't even finished. I knew you were the one when you brought me a tote bag full of books when we first met in person! Thank you for believing in me and my vision for this collection and for ensuring it was in the best shape it could be for submission. You are the best agent I could have ever asked for and it's been such a beautiful journey with you alongside me as my champion and cheerleader. I'm excited for the future – Sian and Shani to the worldddd!

My fairy godsis, Bolu Babalola! Who knew that a viral tweet of my colour-coordinated bookshelf (featuring *Love in Colour* on my display shelf) would lead to me sliding into your DMs?! Thank you so much for your kindness and wisdom, and for introducing me to Juliet Pickering, who introduced me to Sian! Thank you also for being an inspiration and for providing a blueprint for debut short-story authors. You are amazing.

ACKNOWLEDGEMENTS

To my wonderful editor, Juliet Mabey, thank you for making my dream of getting a book deal come true. Thank you for your careful eye and for challenging me to make the manuscript stronger. I am grateful for your patience and for reminding me that I am only a debut author once. You are an absolute legend and it's been a joy working with you.

Thank you to everyone at Oneworld for helping to bring *For Such a Time as This* to life. Thank you especially to Polly Hatfield for your additional comments and edits on my manuscript, to Lucy Cooper and Mary Hawkins in marketing and my publicist Kate Appleton. Thank you also to Clémence Gouy for the stunning illustration and Hayley Warnham for the book cover design. I never really gave much thought to what the cover would look like (other than it having an element of my favourite colour, mustard), but it is perfect. It's been such a wholesome experience working with you all for my first book and I am so grateful. Thank you also to my copy editor Sarah Terry – I had no idea I had a tendency to repeat so many words!

To those in the writing community who have been such godsends on this road to publication, thank you all for your encouragement, mentorship and generosity: Irenosen Okojie, A.M. Dassu, Alexis Keir, Davina Tijani, Nadine Matheson, Yvonne Battle-Felton, Lizzie Damilola Blackburn, Rachel Faturoti, Ore Agbaje-Williams, Tomi Oyemakinde, Marcelle Mateki Akita, Jendella Benson, Sussie Anie, Elizabeth Uviebinené and Caleb Azumah

Nelson (thank you, Caleb, for inspiring me to experiment with the second person). A very special thank you to Bernardine Evaristo. Meeting you at the Woolwich Centre in 2019 changed my life – I realised that writing was the one thing that made sense to me. Thank you for being such an advocate for new writers and for encouraging me to never give up.

And to all of the other authors that inspire me to be a better writer, thank you for sharing your gift with the world: Yaa Gyasi, Brit Bennett, Akwaeke Emezi, Tayari Jones, Taiye Selasi, Jacqueline Crooks, Jyoti Patel, Avni Doshi, Marlon James, Kei Miller, Chimamanda Ngozi Adichie, Abi Daré, Tia Williams, Andrea Levy, Toni Morrison, Nicole Dennis-Benn, Tomi Adeyemi, and (debut) short-story writers: Alexis Arthurs, Nana Kwame Adjei-Brenyah, Deesha Philyaw and Zalika Reid-Benta. Also shout-out to the books, resources and individuals informative in the development of my morning reading and writing practice: *The Slight Edge* (Jeff Olson), *The Practice* (Seth Godin), productivity app Forest and videos by motivational speaker Eric Thomas. And to the authors who had an impact on me during my childhood and teenage years: Trish Cooke, Malorie Blackman, Jacqueline Wilson and Benjamin Zephaniah (rest in perfect peace), thank you.

Thank you to all of the organisations and individuals that have supported me in developing my craft: Spread the Word (especially Ruth Harrison and Aliya Gulamani), The Literary Consultancy, Writing on the Wall, Black Girl Writers, the writing events hosted by Black Ballad and the online work-shops run by Nikesh Shukla during lockdown. A very special thanks to City Lit, especially Vicky Grut's short-story course and the advanced fiction workshop run by Amita Murray in 2020. Amita, thank you for helping me to hone my writing and for reminding me to tell my truth. Thank you also to everyone who was in Amita's workshop and subsequent writing groups, and for all the feedback given on my stories. Thank you to Ollie Charles and everyone else at Untitled Writing for publishing my very first short story and for creating a platform to showcase under-represented writers. To all the superstars in the book world who I have met online over the years, thank you for all of the advice you have given me in navigating the industry, especially Nancy Adimora, Katie Packer, Amy Baxter, Magdalene Abraha, Niki Igbaroola, Sara-Jade Virtue and Elise Dillsworth.

To my wonderful friends who love me so well. Thank you for walking me on this journey and for all of your support over the years, from morning check-ins and encouraging me to start my day at 5 a.m., to spontaneous brunches, prayer calls, cards and flowers to mark key mile-stones. Special shout-out to Serene, Elizabeth, Sarah, Danielle, Carl, Akil, Sanaa, Esther and Anthony. I appreci-ate you guys so much. To my mentors in life generally over the years, Tunji, Andy, Ani, Simon, Michelle, Lena, Dean, Deepak, Bankey, and OF COURSE my big sisters Rachel and Kemi (honestly so blessed to have you both), thank you so much for all of your guidance and wisdom. To my work Gs turned dear friends: Tracy, Yemi, Rebekah and Ope, thank you for being there during the highs and lows of the workplace and reminding me that making my dream of becoming a published author was always something that I could achieve. And to everyone in all of the group chats - over the years, you guys are the best!

Thank you to my first readers, Sarah, Akil, Rebekah, Elizabeth and Serene. Thank you especially to Caleb B and Esther for always reading my stories. To everyone who helped with the research and checking for authenticity in the collection – Dru, Rebekah, Steph, Toyosi, Kelechi, Caleb B, Nigel, Anita, Michael, Emmanuel AA, Ekay, Daniel, Isaac, Ali, Tracy, Fred, Ire, Esther, Sanaa, Rio, Luke, Akil, Sarah and Serene, thank you so much!

To everyone who was involved in the Nyah Network, what a special time we had. Thank you to everyone who attended a book club, a social or a brunch. A special special thank you to Gabriella, Toyosi and Ashley for being such an amazing team.

To everyone who contributed to Chapter 21, my campaign to raise £21,000 in twenty-one days to study my master's in African Studies at Oxford, thank you for investing in my future. To all of my amazing English teachers at Plumstead Manor School, especially Ms Bristow, Ms Martin, and Mr Allan – Sir, I never got to say thank you helping me to get an A* for my English Language GCSE,

ACKNOWLEDGEMENTS

thank you so much! To my Sunday School (E.N.E.R.G.Y) teachers Aunty Ruth, Aunty Sylvia, Aunty Valerie, Aunty Ronica, Colin and so many others, thank you for all of the time you invested in me and so many other young people. You have contributed to the woman I am today. Thank you to those who have become family through the various church communities I have been part of, especially the community like no other at Mile End New Testament Church of God. Thank you, Lucy, for the word you gave me about my writing in January 2020.

To those who have crossed over, Grandad Reggie, Uncle Joel, Uncle Mario, and my godparents Aunty Norma, Uncle Tony, Uncle Godfrey, thank you for the sunshine that you were on earth. I miss you dearly.

To everyone who has followed me on socials over the years for my book content, thank you so much for the love and support. Big up Bookstagram every single time! To Black British (Christian) Twitter, I'm so grateful for all of the many friends I've made and the moments of joy and laughter, especially during lockdown.

And lastly, thank you, reader, for taking the time to read my book and these acknowledgements (basically another short story). I appreciate you so much. May the Lord bless you and keep you and may His face shine upon you.

SA xx

© Jon Osibo

Shani Akilah is a Black British Caribbean writer and screenwriter from South London. She is a book influencer, co-founded the Nyah Network, a book club for Black women, and was a literary judge for the Nota Bene Prize 2023. Shani has a master's degree in African Studies from the University of Oxford. *For Such a Time as This* is her debut short-story collection.